Christian stared at the woman before him

He wanted to tell her how beautiful she looked, but he couldn't—or wouldn't.

He stepped toward her, and she didn't stop him. Her eyes widened and the tip of her tongue darted out to moisten her lips. The small motion nearly caused his knees to buckle. "I have a confession to make," he began, his voice straining as his body tightened.

"And what would that be?" she asked, her eyes wide and luminous.

Instead of answering, he simply brushed a soft yet firm kiss against the sweetness of her mouth. Once his lips touched hers the contact ignited a firestorm that he couldn't quite control. Her body melted against his, pressing in all the right places. Her softness fit perfectly against his hardened planes, and as she clutched his lower back, he felt his whole world tilt.

Of course, this complicated matters.

Dear Reader,

Sometimes life doesn't turn out the way we envision. A series of bad judgments can derail the most focused individual, sending them crashing into a situation that wasn't of their design and certainly not part of their dreams. When Skye D'Lane materialized in my mind, I knew her soul before I ever knew her story. She's the tough but tender, not-going-to-give-up heroine who finds love and acceptance in the arms of a truly amazing man—Christian Holt.

This story is near and dear to my heart, as I believe in the power of self-love and forgiveness. We've all stumbled and made mistakes, but it takes a strong will to pull yourself up and keep going even if no one else believes you can.

I hope you enjoy this story of redemption and forgiveness tempered with love. I know I did!

Don't miss the last in the Mama Jo's Boys trilogy next month, *Secrets in a Small Town.*

Hearing from readers is one of my greatest joys. Feel free to drop me a line at my website, www.kimberlyvanmeter.com, or through snail mail at P.O. Box 2210, Oakdale, CA 95361.

Happy reading,

Kimberly Van Meter

A Chance in the Night

Kimberly Van Meter

TORONTO NEW YORK LONDON
AMSTERDAM PARIS SYDNEY HAMBURG
STOCKHOLM ATHENS TOKYO MILAN MADRID
PRAGUE WARSAW BUDAPEST AUCKLAND

Recycling programs for this product may not exist in your area.

ISBN-13: 978-0-373-71700-2

A CHANCE IN THE NIGHT

This edition published by arrangement with Harlequin Books S.A.

For questions and comments about the quality of this book please contact us at Customer_eCare@Harlequin.ca.

www.eHarlequin.com

Printed in U.S.A.

ABOUT THE AUTHOR

Kimberly Van Meter wrote her first book at age sixteen and finally achieved publication in December 2006. She writes for Harlequin Superromance and Harlequin Romantic Suspense. She and her husband of seventeen years have three children, three cats and always a houseful of friends, family and fun.

Books by Kimberly Van Meter

HARLEQUIN SUPERROMANCE

1391—THE TRUTH ABOUT FAMILY
1433—FATHER MATERIAL*
1469—RETURN TO EMMETT'S MILL*
1485—A KISS TO REMEMBER*
1513—AN IMPERFECT MATCH*
1577—KIDS ON THE DOORSTEP*
1600—A MAN WORTH LOVING*
1627—TRUSTING THE BODYGUARD*
1694—THE PAST BETWEEN US**

*Home in Emmett's Mill
**Mama Jo's Boys

HARLEQUIN ROMANTIC SUSPENSE

1622—TO CATCH A KILLER
1638—GUARDING THE SOCIALITE

To anyone who's found the courage
to pick themselves up after a devastating
fall...take pride in your courage
and your refusal to quit.
You are an inspiration!

CHAPTER ONE

CHRISTIAN HOLT KNEW THE minute she entered the bar. His skin prickled in a sensation that was not unpleasant but certainly unnerving as his subconscious seemed to be on high alert for this particular woman and he wished he could find the off switch.

He didn't want to notice how her hair waved like summer wheat in a soft breeze over a gently rounded shoulder or how her face reminded him of an artist's rendition of Helen of Troy that he saw in an art gallery in Soho.

A businessman wearing a Brioni suit flagged him with a lifted finger and ordered a Bombay Sapphire gin and tonic. Christian could tell by the six-thousand dollar threads the man was going to ask for the good stuff. He could also tell that the man wasn't a good tipper by the way he didn't make eye contact with him, as if Christian was beneath his notice. Christian gave the man his drink and, as expected, the businessman barely gave him ten percent. Christian smiled and nodded to the man for his patronage and then made a mental note to go light on the booze next round.

Unbidden, Christian's gaze returned to where the

woman was sitting. She wasn't what he'd call a regular at Martini, the upscale Manhattan bar where he'd worked for the past three years, as she rarely drank but she was there often enough for him to notice why she came.

Martini, for all its elegance and refinement, was an excellent feeding ground for anyone with a rich palate. It was a playground for the wealthy and overprivileged, with its posh contemporary decor backlit by hidden lighting. He watched as money changed hands, deals were sealed with predatory smiles and beautiful women were never far from the action.

And this woman, with her perfect figure and equally perfect face, was one of many he saw slinking around the city for one purpose: another's entertainment.

He slewed his gaze away from her, disgust threatening to curl his lip and ruin the careful facade he put out there as the amiable professional who knew when to look away and when to quietly pay attention.

He wanted nothing to do with this woman. Or any woman of her profession.

Christian had an eye for detail that he'd honed on the raw situations that shaped his early childhood. Out of necessity he'd learned how to read people as well as any FBI profiler with a fancy education. He'd learned his skills on the streets, figuring out quite young that everyone had something to hide and sometimes those secrets were vile enough to twist a person into something ugly. So, yeah, Christian had a sixth sense about people. And he was using those skills to make a nice living as a bartender at Martini where money was no object and anything could be bought.

Including the woman at the end of the bar.

Still, as much as he schooled his gaze away from her, she crept into his thoughts as if he had a giant magnet buried in his forehead tugging him in her direction.

A busty redhead took a seat at the bar and he smiled on autopilot. "Let me guess…white wine spritzer," he said, and her smile widened.

"How'd you know?" she asked, her appraising look taking careful yet casual note of his person and liking what she saw. He knew if he played it right he could get her number easily but he wasn't hunting for a good time tonight. Besides, there was too much of a distraction in his peripheral vision to truly focus on the delights of the woman in front of him.

He grinned with a shrug. "Lucky guess."

"I almost ordered a vodka martini," she said, the corners of her mouth lifting into a flirtier smile.

He cocked his head in thought. "Ah, but something tells me you're not a martini drinker and the only reason you were considering it was because you heard that Martini had the best ones in town and you wanted to try it out," he surmised to her delight, prompting him to continue. "*And,* if you had your preference, you'd ditch the spritzer altogether and order the champagne but you're saving that for your date." *So he can pay for it.*

She laughed, leaning forward in a subtle, yet playful motion that gave him an unobstructed view of her double D's as she said, "You're good. Are you psychic or something?"

He winked. "I'll never tell." But if he were psychic he'd know all the details about the woman at the end of the bar, whether he wanted to or not. And as much as he tried to ignore it, his curiosity was becoming an irritant. He returned to the woman in front of him and gestured to the door as a man entered and scanned the bar. "That your friend?"

She glanced toward the entrance and barely hid her disappointment, which told him he'd been right again. He handed her the spritzer and she reluctantly slid from the bar stool. "See you around," she said, and he just smiled. She left with a suggestive "Maybe sooner rather than later" and walked away slowly so as to give Christian ample time to check out her perfectly sculpted ass. Any other time he'd have enjoyed the view but his gaze returned to the woman he was trying to ignore.

Tonight, there was something different about her. It was subtle to be sure but there was a dark edge to her that bordered on despair, or perhaps desperation. The fingers on her left hand trembled as she played with the base of her wineglass, the white wine she'd ordered earlier untouched. Every now and again, her gaze would drift over the crowd; she was clearly waiting for someone. He noted the barest sense of relief each time her sweep revealed nothing. Whoever she was waiting for wasn't someone whose attention she wanted.

Occupational hazard, he supposed.

He ought to inquire if the wine wasn't to her liking, seeing as she hadn't tasted the pinot grigio since ordering it but he was reluctant to engage in conversation with her, even if only superficially. There were plenty of times he chatted with the regulars, flirted with the cougars and even hooked up a time or two with a hot patron looking for a good time with no strings attached, but he didn't want to create any kind of familiarity with the woman at the end of the bar.

But, she drew him just the same. Something in her life was putting the subtle wrinkle in her otherwise smooth brow and something was causing her to perch rigidly on her chair, looking brittle enough to crack with a touch. Oh, but she was doing a damn fine job of hiding whatever was eating at her. He had to give her that but he saw beyond her efforts and he wasn't happy about it. Sometimes his keen sense about people was a burden he didn't enjoy carrying.

Like right now.

His feet threatened to carry him in her direction but fate intervened and a portly man appeared at her side, eagerness and hunger in his eyes, and Christian faded to the far side of the bar. He had no wish to witness the beginning of the soulless transaction between the two. He knew that she would leave with the fat man because he had paid her to.

Christian's mouth tightened as a different memory intruded.

Men—not quite so refined in their tastes or heavy in their pocketbook—bursting through the door of the motel where he played with his action figures. Old fat men or young strung-out men, their hands shoved up his mother's blouse, squeezing her breasts and grunting with anticipation as they tumbled to the bed.

"Christian baby, go get yourself a soda or something," she instructed breathlessly, the hot, feverish glaze of her eyes burning into him as he bolted for the door. He knew the drill. His mom would need at least an hour to get the job done.

He closed his eyes and shut the door behind him, wishing he could wipe away that image—and a hundred others before it—and jump into someone else's life where moms didn't earn the rent money on their backs, home wasn't a sleazy motel on the bad side of town and hunger didn't follow you like an unwelcome shadow because there was never enough to eat.

Christian came back to the present with a jerk, annoyed that such a crappy memory had burst free from his mental lockbox. He never thought of those days anymore. His life before eleven years of age was shitty enough the first go round, he didn't need to revisit it in memory. His gaze found the woman as she left the bar, grace personified on the man's arm, and muttered a curse under his breath.

He didn't care what her problems were.

And there was nothing that could make him care.

SKYE D'LANE TRIED HARD not to stiffen and arch away from the touch of her date as his palm burned a hole into her lower back as they walked to the awaiting Town Car idling at the curb.

Her thoughts returned to the bartender at Martini. He'd make a good escort, she thought wryly. Rich women would no doubt pay a good sum to get their manicured hands on his lean body. She was surprised Belleni hadn't gotten a hold of him yet. Belleni had a way of drawing in the beautiful ones; it's what made him so powerful. He offered the best to his clients and they paid him well for the privilege of booking a date with Belleni's elite stable. She remembered when Belleni had approached her, his benign smile hiding a multitude of sins, and she'd fallen for the easy lies that he parceled out like fine morsels to a starving person.

She'd been broken inside and he'd capitalized on it. Before she knew it, she'd been snared by a net of her own making.

Dreams were a dangerous thing in New York, Manhattan specifically. The glitz could blind you. She should know. She resisted the urge to massage the phantom ache in her knee that always bloomed when she thought of her own hopes and dreams. The injury had healed but her career as a professional dancer had not.

She resigned herself to an evening that by the end, she knew she'd want to forget.

She tried to find that place inside of herself that enabled her to forget what she was about to do and pretend to be the gracious, accommodating escort to whomever had paid the exorbitant price Belleni required for her services, but tonight it eluded her. Her fingers shook as she clasped her beaded clutch, swallowing as she squeezed her eyes shut for a brief second, reaching desperately for that inner strength but her conversation with Belleni only an hour earlier kept coming back to her, shattering her calm.

He was never going to let her go. Not while she remained his Number One girl. Belleni's hold on her was resolute. He held her most precious possession as collateral.

Nico.

Their four-year-old son.

Skye exhaled softly as the maddening ache of despair arced through her and she knew she had to put that aside for the moment. Her date—Carlton Essex III—wanted Skye D'Lane, gorgeous, sophisticated, with a willing disposition, on his arm and likely, in his bed by the end of the evening if the price was right. The thought caused bile to sear her throat but she gave no indication of her true feelings.

"You do not disappoint, Miss D'Lane," Carlton

murmured into her ear as the car pulled away, his hand resting a bit too closely to her inner thigh. The eagerness in his voice was downright disgusting. His gaze drifted over her silver metallic sheath and his breathing quickened.

"Neither do you," she lied easily, hoping the evening ended soon. The client had booked her for a charity event at the Four Seasons where he would be donating a large sum to a center for rehabilitated prostitutes. Skye found the irony sickening, though she supposed in her own small way she was helping, too.

"Your skin is like smooth silk," he said, his tongue sliding along his lower lip as if he were already tasting her. She withheld a shudder. This one would likely leave marks on her tender breasts. In a perverse way, she hoped he would. Belleni didn't take it lightly when a client left marks on his girls; healing time caused downtime and downtime cost Belleni money. He began running his hand up her thigh, slowly lifting the hem of her dress. "So perfect…"

She wanted to scream *Don't touch me, you filthy pig,* but instead she simply laughed and gave his hand a gentle nudge with a smile she didn't feel and reminded him of the rules. "I'm sure Belleni explained our arrangement, yes?"

Carlton narrowed his already beady eyes and drew back with a displeased grunt. "No touching in public," he answered. He paused a minute to adjust his girth in the well-tailored suit but his gaze skewed back to her with a glint that she didn't trust as he said, "But we're not in public and I want a preview of what I paid for."

So crass. It was no wonder the man—as wealthy as he was—had to pay someone for company let alone sex. She managed a light laugh. "So impatient. The anticipation will sweeten the experience. We wouldn't want to be late to your event."

"They'll wait. I want to see why you're Belleni's most expensive whore."

She didn't like the hard light in his eyes. Malice rolled off him in waves. Her pulse quickened as she considered her options. She chose her words carefully. "There are rules to follow if you don't wish to find yourself on Belleni's bad side," she warned him, hoping it was enough to cool the hot lust in his stare.

But Carlton didn't heed her warning. Hell, the subtle threat seemed to incite him further. He jerked her to him in a swift movement that Skye would've thought impossible given his size, squeezing a pained gasp from her even as she pushed against him. "What are you doing?" she tried demanding with some sort of authority, but in truth, fear had replaced her calm bravado. "This isn't the way Belleni does business. You're risking more than you know if you don't follow the rules."

He ignored her and directed his driver to pull around to the back of the bar, out of sight, tucked into the dark alley. His grip tightened on her flesh as her sheath rode up, exposing her rear. He tossed her to the seat and wasted little time in covering her body with his considerable girth. Oh, God, he was going to crush her. She pushed against him, panic fighting with her need to remain in control of the situation for her own sake.

"Please don't..." she gasped.

His breath hot on her face, his thick hands groping under her dress, bruising the flesh as he sought the tender folds, caused her to react in pure instinct as she raked her fingers down his face hard enough to draw blood. He grunted in shocked pain, drawing away a fraction, giving her more room to breathe and wiggle away from him but while the Town Car was roomier than the standard sedan, Carlton's bulk made it difficult to maneuver far. She reached for the door but before her hand could touch the handle, he hauled her back with his fist tangled in her long hair.

"You bitch," he growled in her ear, his grip tight at her scalp. She twisted against his hold, blinking back tears of pain, refusing to give him what the sadistic bastard wanted. His lips stretched in an ugly knowing smile as he held her captive, helpless and scared. "You've been a bad girl. I like that. But you've made a mark on my face. Only I'm allowed to leave marks." He drove his fist into her belly, the shock and agony of it causing her to suck air. Heaven help her, he was going to beat her, maybe even kill her. He didn't care about the consequences.

"B-belleni will have your balls," she managed to choke out but Carlton just laughed.

"You're a whore. Easily bought and easily replaced," he responded with a shrug, shredding her designer sheath to expose her breasts.

"S-stop," she shrieked, true fear blotting out rational thought as she frantically tried to cover herself. She'd never been in such a situation before. Belleni only allowed select clientele to book his girls. Never before had she been paired with such a monster. She knew how to deal with overeager clients, not ones with a sadistic streak. Her phone and pepper spray were in her clutch, which had fallen to the floor when he'd thrown her. She twisted and reached desperately for her clutch but a lightning-fast crack across her jaw caused stars to fly around her head and black dots to pulse before her eyes.

"You're a feisty one," she heard him murmur, the appreciative tone sickening her. "Let's see if you're worth what I paid."

Blood filled her mouth from her busted lip but she opened her mouth and screamed for all she was worth. Someone, oh, God, please help her.

CHRISTIAN HAD JUST STEPPED into the alley behind Martini to take his break when he stopped short at the muffled scream coming from the sleek Town Car that lurked in the shadows. The violent rock of the Town Car betrayed a tussle and by the sounds of it, a woman was involved. His brain directed him to return to the bar. It was best to remain uninvolved. The last thing he needed was to get tangled up in someone else's business. But even as he turned, his hand reaching for the handle, his conscience balked. What if the woman was really getting brutalized? Could he live with himself if something bad happened to her? No. However, the logical side of his brain countered, what if it's just some kinky couple who liked it rough and she's in no real danger after all? Busting in on someone's private time would only cause embarrassment all around.

The logical argument pulled considerable weight but as another scream sounded from the interior only to be cut suspiciously short, he said, "Screw it," to the logical side of his brain and bounded for the car. But even as he told himself he'd deal with the ramifications of his actions later, he was shocked when he jerked open the door and saw the woman from the bar, bleeding and struggling feebly against the hulking mass on top of her, choking the life out of her.

CHAPTER TWO

"WHAT THE F—" THE FAT MAN startled as Christian reached inside the car and dragged him out and off the woman who looked in bad shape. He landed a solid punch to the man's flabby, jowled face, knocking him to the ground, howling. The driver erupted from the car and trained a gun on him, the subtle shake in his grip betraying the fact that he'd probably never fired the thing, but it didn't make Christian feel any less freaked that he was staring down the business end of a 9mm.

"Don't do it, man," he warned. "You've got a half-dead woman in your car right now and you don't want to add more misery to your plate. I doubt your piece of shit employer is paying you well enough to cover up murder. Think about it. It ain't worth it. I'm going to get the girl and we're all going to walk away nice and easy."

The driver gave a short nod as the fat man lumbered to his feet, wiping at the blood flowing from his nose. "Take the bitch. I'm through with her," he said, his voice nasal and wet sounding. His lip curled in disgust. "Tell Belleni I want my money back. His whore wasn't worth the asking price," he said, mistaking Christian for someone affiliated with the woman and her business. That alone made him want to further rearrange the asshole's face but he settled for a hard-edged glare at the man as he edged past him to gingerly pull the woman from the vehicle, cradling her against his chest.

With a curt nod to his driver, the fat man disappeared into the Town Car and slammed the door behind him as the car melted into the night.

He glanced down at the woman in his arms. She was badly beaten. Blood dribbled from her nose and swollen lip, smearing the honey-hued locks he'd noticed at the bar. She was a far cry from the sophisticated trophy that'd been perched on the stool earlier. He couldn't take her into the bar like this. She opened one eye and he could see the glaze of pain. "I need to take you to the hospital," he told her. He wasn't surprised by the weak shake of her head as she moaned.

"No hospital, p-please," she said, laboring for each word. "I'll be…punished." The last part came out with a low sob as she huddled against him and his resolve broke.

Ah, hell. It was his mother all over again. She could be suffering internal injuries and there'd be no way for him to know until it was too late but he knew why she'd rather die than step foot in a hospital because the care came with a price. Hospital staff were required to report if they suspected a patient had been the victim of a violent crime. And if he dragged a broken woman into the E.R., they'd certainly start asking questions. He'd learned that the first time a john had nearly killed his mother. He'd been six and scared. The hospital staff had saved his mother but they'd had to sneak out when the questions had started.

He rolled his eyes to the midnight sky and cursed his own damn luck for sticking his nose where it didn't belong and landing himself a problem he didn't want. Lucky for her, he lived in a loft above the bar. He supposed he could take her there for the time being until he figured out what else to do. He fished his phone from his pocket and dialed his friend Gage Stratham, who was also on the floor that night, telling him that he had an emergency and he needed coverage at the bar. Gage told him he'd take care of it and Christian carried the woman up to his loft.

He managed to open his front door and then close it with a nudge of his foot. The loft was a convenient pad and he'd turned the run-down space into something he didn't mind people seeing but he doubted the woman in his arms cared much about the blond hardwood floors he'd installed himself or the four-poster California King bed with its goose down comforter that he was laying her gently on. After spending eleven years of his childhood in sleazy motels, sleeping on threadbare, worn and often dirty linens, Christian had a taste—no requirement—for fine bedding. He winced at the thought of blood staining the white duvet but he didn't have a choice.

It wasn't like she could manage to wash up on her own right now. He averted his eyes as the ruined dress hung on her slender frame, ripped down the center so that she had little covering her lithe body. Even as he looked away, he'd caught an unfortunate glimpse of creamy, well-toned thighs and near perfect rose-tipped breasts.

He swallowed and then cursed softly. He needed to assess her injuries. He went to his bathroom and pulled out hydrogen peroxide, a clean washcloth, cotton balls and antiseptic cream. He sighed, hating that he even had the knowledge required. After that first episode with his mother, he'd taken over bandaging and administering first aid when johns got a little rough.

He dropped the supplies on his bed beside her and after rummaging through his dresser drawers, he found an old T-shirt he didn't mind parting with and some old sweats she could wear. Her eyes slid open and tears leaked from the corners of her eyes as she understood his intention.

"Thank you," she said in a low voice choked with pain.

"Save the thank-yous for later. This is likely going to hurt like a son of a bitch," he muttered in warning. He wasn't her prince charming coming to rescue her from her life but human decency demanded that he do what he could to help. "Can you sit up?" he asked. She struggled, blanching with the pain as she tried. He gently stopped her. "You might have a broken rib. You really should see a doctor," he admonished but he knew it fell on deaf ears. "I'll do what I can but you're pretty messed up." She gave a subtle nod to indicate she understood but otherwise remained silent. He swabbed the crusting blood from her jawline and wiped the matted strands of her hair. "Did you know him?" he asked, telling himself he wasn't interested in the answer, he was just filling the space between them with words, perhaps to distract her from the pain. His mother had never known a single man who'd paid for her services. The only man she'd bedded and known was his father and it wasn't as though he'd been a catch. He'd died in prison, serving time for aggravated assault. His biological family tree wasn't anything to write home about. "You ought to file charges," he suggested, dabbing her lip with antibiotic cream. She winced and he gentled his touch, a familiar well of frustration lacing his tone as he added, "If you don't, at least tell the authorities. He might do this to someone else. Maybe a friend of yours or something."

"I don't have any friends," she responded, in a voice so scratchy he barely made out the words.

Then he saw the finger bruises along her throat. That man had nearly killed her, not figuratively, but literally. Another occupational hazard, he thought bitterly. He couldn't understand her choice to lower herself in such a way. "You're a beautiful woman. There are other choices out there. Hell, find yourself some sugar daddy and become his arm candy but at least get the ring on your finger so you have some kind of security if he ditches you for another." He threw the soiled cotton swabs in the bedside trash and steeled himself for what came next. "Listen, I promise to do this quick," he said, lifting the shirt in his hand. "But we gotta get you into some real clothes. Okay?" She nodded and he tried to gently pull off the remains of her dress without hurting her. "Here," he said gruffly, sliding the T over her head as carefully as possible. He made quick work of tugging his faded sweats up her legs. They hung on her slight frame but at least they covered her. He released a short breath he didn't realize he'd been holding and rose, saying, "I'll get you some Tylenol. I'm not big on meds so it's the best I can do."

He didn't wait for her acknowledgment or, frankly, for anything, he simply bolted for the bathroom. He needed a minute to collect himself. His mother had been a street prostitute. She hadn't slept on five hundred thread count sheets or enjoyed caviar and champagne. Not like the woman on his bed. She had the look of someone who knew all about fine living. Everything about her seemed delicate and fragile, refined and expensive. Yet, just like his mother, she sold herself for cold, hard cash.

In that they were the same. And for that reason, he couldn't—wouldn't—allow any kind of deep connection to take root.

When he finally left the bathroom, a few Tylenol

tablets in his hand and a glass of water, he'd managed to put his emotions back in order.

He helped her with the painkillers and covered her with a blanket. "Is there someone I should call?" he asked, not quite able to bring himself to say the word *pimp.* Her bruised throat worked as she swallowed and he knew it must hurt like hell. That fat bastard had really done a number on her. She shook her head and he sighed. "Well—" he gestured to the bed "—you're welcome to stay the night. I'll take the couch."

"Thank you," she said again, and he was no more ready to accept her gratitude now than he was the first go-round but Mama Jo, his foster mother, had drilled manners into his head since the day he'd shown up on her doorstep, courtesy of the Bridgeport, West Virginia foster system so many years ago.

"Yeah, sure," he muttered, taking his pillow and blanket to the couch. "Don't mention it. Get some rest."

Something told him sleep would find her sooner than it would him.

SKYE AWOKE TO A PARADE of pain. Her rib was most certainly broken on her left side. Early morning shafts of sunlight streamed into the loft, bathing everything in a soft creamy light that would've been beautiful if she hadn't been sucking back tears at the agony in her body. Just breathing took effort.

As she slowly took stock of her situation, she

remembered the details from the night. That corpulent pig—Carlton Essex III—had done this to her. She'd been unable to get to her phone or her pepper spray. And Carlton had been unconcerned by the threat of displeasing Belleni. In that the man was an idiot. Belleni was vicious when crossed.

Her gaze slid over to the sofa where soft snoring sounded. She rolled to her uninjured side, nearly crying out at the bite of pain, and slowly stood. She spied her clutch and the remains of her Anna Sui sheath. She grabbed the clutch but left the dress and made her way to the door. The man—she didn't even known his name—didn't stir even as she padded slowly to the door. She regretted leaving like this after he'd taken her in but Belleni was probably turning the city upside down looking for her and she'd rather not repay the man's kindness by dragging him further into the mess that was her life. There was also her mangled pride in her reasoning, as well. How could she adequately express her gratitude to someone for saving her from someone she'd been paid to service? Shame twisted her guts in a knot and she slipped from the loft with only the hope that karma would find the man still sleeping and repay him appropriately for his kindness.

God knew she couldn't.

CHAPTER THREE

CHRISTIAN WOKE WITH A SNAP of his eyes, knowing without having to look that she was gone. Still, he rose and swore under his breath when he confirmed the suspicion. This was good, he told himself when irritation followed at the knowledge she'd snuck out while he slept. Now he didn't have to deal with the inevitable awkwardness of the morning after, not the typical *morning after* mind you, but it would have been weird considering what had happened.

He walked to his bed and saw that she'd taken her little purse but left her dress behind. He lifted the ruined mess from the floor and her scent wafted from the material. The dress was cool against his fingers as he replayed the scenario from last night in his head. Questions nagged at him but he resigned himself to letting them go. She was gone. It was probably better this way. Christian tossed the dress into the trash, noting with wry humor, that scrap of silk had material that probably cost more than some people saw in a month's wages. And now it was in his trash. Somehow that seemed sadly metaphoric. His brothers had always accused him of having the heart of a poet. Seems they weren't wrong. Damn.

He sighed and headed for the shower and hoped for a day that was devoid of mystery women, their questionable choices in life and rich, well-dressed pricks.

SKYE SANK LOWER IN THE HOT water, the details from the night too fresh in her mind, and closed her eyes. Steam rose and drifted from her body as she allowed the heat to soak into her bones.

A tear slipped down her cheek and she winced as the pain reminded her of what had gone down only hours before.

Some men were rutting bastards who found excitement in the pain of others. She swallowed and wiped away the tear. He'd done more than leave just bruises. She touched the swollen flesh of her upper lip and winced. The doctor Belleni kept on the payroll confirmed the broken rib and gave her some painkillers with the advice to rest.

"He will not touch you again," a voice at the door vowed, making her tense beneath the water. She opened her eyes to see Belleni standing in the doorway, gazing at her body as if he had the right. "The man was a pig but no worries, darling, he has enjoyed his last Belleni girl, I assure you."

She slid the washcloth over her breasts as a slow, quiet rage percolated in her chest at the liberties he took just because he believed she belonged to him. "I want to be alone, Belleni," she said, hating the way his gaze roamed her nakedness, resting on areas that belonged to no man, least of all him. But even as she burned to tell him to get the hell out of her life, she was held captive by a past she couldn't change.

Instead of complying with the curt response, he settled himself at the edge of the bathtub with an indulgent smile. He was a good-looking older man with an air of experience that was misleading in its seeming benevolence. Even as she loathed him, sometimes it was hard to separate her tangled feelings, for Nico was his spitting image and she adored her son with single-minded focus. She chose to keep her attention away from his roving stare for fear of her tongue getting the best of her. Still, she fairly vibrated with the tempest raging inside her over her inability to extricate herself and Nico from Belleni's sphere of influence and she didn't trust what might fly from her mouth.

"You are angry," he surmised, his Italian accent smooth as fine liquor, his touch deceptively gentle on her cheek. She pulled away and he sighed. "Of course, you are. And you have every right to be. I should've listened to my instincts, no matter the hefty weight of his bank account. Can you forgive me, my love?" he asked, his gaze softening with an emotion Skye knew didn't exist in his world. She choked down the bitterness stuck in her throat and nodded but the effort nearly killed her. Belleni smiled. "Good. But I must make amends to my best girl. While you heal I shall see to it that you want for nothing. You will have the best of care. Name it and you shall have it. But first, tell me how you managed to get away from this brute? Vincent said you didn't call him for help."

She wouldn't give up her kind stranger. She wished she'd gotten his name but she recognized that it was better this way. She would likely never see him again as she planned to avoid Martini from here on out after the whole experience. Still, she found herself thinking of him and his kindness to her when she shouldn't be thinking of him at all. "I sprayed him with pepper spray," she lied. "Then I called a cab and came here."

He eyed her with faint suspicion. She held her breath as more questions built behind his speculative stare. "What are you going to do to him?" she asked, hoping to distract Belleni from his current train of thought.

Belleni waved away her question. "The details are unnecessary for you to know at this point. Just take me at my word that he will pay for his insult. Now name your desire, my love, and I will see to it personally."

She knew he awaited her gratitude but she couldn't make herself utter the words. He expected her to thank him for taking care of her when he was the one who had set her up with that monster? It was his fault her lip was split and her eye was blackened. Her breasts were marked with bruises from where the man had squeezed so hard tears sprang to her eyes at the memory. Her neck still bore the finger marks from where he tried to choke her to death. He hadn't been interested in straight sex. No, he'd wanted to hurt and because he'd paid a good sum for her services, he'd believed he could do what he wanted with her. And he nearly had. Belleni heaved a sad sigh and rose from the tub's edge. "It pains me to see you so abused. I will make this up to you, my darling," he promised.

She stared at the tips of her toes as they peeked from the water's edge where she rested her feet against the water spigot. "You mean it?" she asked softly.

"Of course, what do you desire and I will make it yours," he said.

"I want Nico home with me." She turned and met his gaze with her one eye that wasn't impeded by swollen tissue and said, "He shouldn't live with you and Vivian. He should live with his mother."

At her quiet request Belleni hardened into the man she knew hid under that soft and generous exterior. Gone was the loving benefactor, former lover and father of her son, replaced in a heartbeat by the man's true character that was obsessed with her and ruthless in his determination to keep her at all costs. "He stays with me," he said brusquely. "You have had a hard night. I will forgive you. But do not try me, darling. I would not have you attempt something brash. You must remember that I am not a fool," he reminded her, straightening his cuffs with slow, methodical movements that betrayed his need for control in all things. "Get your rest. We will discuss things further after you've had a chance to think more clearly."

He left her alone and when she heard him leave the apartment, she shuddered and tried to draw a deep breath but the air felt trapped in her lungs. There was nothing she didn't understand with the clarity of glass. Belleni knew if he didn't keep Nico she'd try to run again.

She'd tried to run away when Nico was born but Belleni's watchdog, Vivian, had caught her as she'd tried to board the train. Belleni's punishment had been to take Nico from her physically. She hadn't even been allowed to breastfeed her own child any longer. At six weeks old Nico had been taken from her breast and put on a bottle. The punishment had served its purpose. The second time she'd tried to run, Nico had been two years old. Vivian had found a credit card receipt for airfare out of the city. Her punishment for that had been even worse. Belleni had kept her son from her for three months. By the time he'd allowed her to see Nico, her son had nearly forgotten her. Belleni had known the effect it would have on her when Nico shied away from her open arms and returned to cling to Belleni's leg.

The pain had been unimaginable.

This time, she'd thought she'd get away.

Everything she'd worked for, all the money she'd managed to squirrel away…useless and for nothing. Her future stretched out before her in an endless road of servitude and the magnitude of her despair drowned the last ounce of hope she'd been fostering since the day Nico was born.

"Oh, baby," she whispered as a wave of shame overtook her. She couldn't go backward and she couldn't move forward. She was permanently stuck under Belleni's thumb. Tears burned her eyes and she didn't have the strength to hold them back any longer…so she didn't.

IT'D BEEN A WEEK SINCE the incident with the mystery woman but that coupled with the other things on his mind had served to cripple Christian's REM time, leaving him grouchy and fatigued by morning. He rose early in spite of having hit the sheets only a few hours prior and went to the gym. Christian melted into the busy streets and walked the short distance to his local fitness center. He felt like crap, the lack of sleep was really starting to wear on him, but there was more to his edge than fatigue. His buddy and business partner Gage had been pressuring him to take a meeting with this bigwig money guy so they could finally open their own nightclub, but Christian wasn't warm to the idea of bringing more people to the deal. That saying "Too many cooks in the kitchen…" came to mind and he could almost hear his foster mother's voice in his head saying it, too. Mama Jo may be a couple of states away in West Virginia but her voice was firmly in his subconscious. Most times, it was a good thing because it kept him walking the straight and narrow when he might otherwise feel pulled in a different direction. Other times it was a bit annoying to have the female version of Jiminy Cricket on his shoulder.

He entered the fitness center and was met by loud music and a tattooed woman who looked as if she could bench-press him without breaking a sweat. She smiled, revealing her tongue piercing—something Christian had never found attractive—but he returned the smile as he swiped his membership ID.

Christian met Gage at the weight station where he was already doing his reps.

"You're late," Gage said, his face tightening with the exertion of a curling exercise set with major poundage.

Christian pulled his sweatshirt over his head and tossed it aside. "Cut me some slack. I just went to bed about three hours ago. You're lucky I came at all."

Gage grunted and allowed the weight to slowly release. "Yeah, yeah, cry me a river." He grabbed a towel and mopped his face. "So, you give any more thought to what I mentioned to you the other day?" he asked, around a gulp of Vitaminwater.

Christian withheld the grimace threatening to pull on his mouth. He knew this was their best shot but it left him with a bad taste. Still, he nodded. "Yeah. I guess I'm in. What do you know about this guy? Is he solid? I don't want to climb into bed with someone who's going to just take my money and split," he grumbled.

Gage brightened and grinned. "So paranoid. Yeah,

he's solid. This is what he does. He handpicks projects to invest in. Trust me, everyone in town wants this guy in their corner."

"So how do you know him?" Christian asked.

Gage shrugged but his expression turned coy. "I just do. This is our best chance at getting the club off the ground in this environment. It's not like we have a handful of investors lining up to open a nightclub in this economic climate. It sucks, man. That's why it's important that you make a good impression with him."

"What's his name again?" Christian asked, settling into the leg press machine.

"Frank Rocco," Gage answered, getting ready for another set. "I think you'll like him. He's a nice older guy who gives off a real down-to-earth vibe. Nothing like the rest of the suits I've dealt with. Frank's the kind of guy who would sit down and have a beer with you just as easily as he would drink some fancy French wine. You'll like him," Gage assured him with another grin. He blew out a short breath and started his sets.

They were both silent for the moment, focused on the exercise, but Christian's mind was not on his reps but rather what he felt was a crossroads in his life. He'd always dreamed of owning his own nightclub, something classy like Martini only not quite so stuffy, but just when he thought he'd saved enough capital to quit his job so he could focus on his own project, he was faced with the unpleasant reality that no one was willing to float him a loan because he had no track record in his field. It was the proverbial catch-22. He needed experience to prove himself but he couldn't prove himself without experience. So he needed someone who was willing to take a chance on him and his vision to get his foot in the door. It'd been a year of trying to find the capital and coming up short that had finally tipped the scale. He didn't like the idea of being attached to a money guy but he was willing to do what it took to get his business open.

"So set up the meeting then," Christian said, his jaw tight.

"Good, because I already did," Gage admitted with a grunt as he lowered the weights, sweat running down his face in rivulets. "First meeting is set for next week over coffee at this little hole-in-the-wall place called Café Au Lait that supposedly makes the best espresso in the Village. Wear something casual but not too casual."

"I know how to dress," Christian said, shooting his friend an annoyed look. "You just worry about yourself. I always make a good first impression."

Gage mopped his face. "You're right. That's why I know this is going to work. I wouldn't have tied myself to you in this deal if I didn't think we could make it happen. I forgot my phone at home so I'll text you the date, time and address when we're done here."

"Thanks," Christian said, appreciating his friend's

candor and his support but it wasn't entirely altruistic on Gage's part. Gage, like Christian, wanted to make money. He finished his set and moved to another machine to work on his deltoids. He focused on the workout, glad to blank out for a minute. The past few weeks had been hell. He loved the city but sometimes it wore him down. It was easy to stumble and fall in this place where the pace never stopped or slowed down for pedestrians. But every now and again, he felt that odd twinge for a little peace and quiet. He usually satisfied that urge with a visit home to Mama Jo but he hadn't been able to get back there for a while now. He knew what the twinge really was—guilt.

Mama Jo had raised him and his foster brothers, Thomas and Owen, when hell had opened its doors for each of them and the flames of their personal lives had threatened to incinerate them.

He owed that woman more than she could ever know. That was another reason he wanted to get the club running. He wanted to make sure he always had the means to take care of Mama Jo if the need ever arose. He knew he could make a go of things if he was given the chance, but so far, he'd been hit by a shitload of roadblocks. And he was feeling the pressure.

"Hey, I need a favor," Gage said, interrupting his thoughts. Christian slowly disengaged the weights and stepped away from the machine he was using, suspicion raising his brows at Gage's request. "I managed to score this date with a girl I've been trying to land for weeks now and she finally said yes..."

Christian shook his head, knowing where this was going. "I don't double-date," he said.

"Dude, wait until you see her friend. She's hot," he assured him but Christian wasn't buying.

"So why aren't you going after her instead?"

"I'm a gentleman—"

"No, you're not. You're a man-whore. What's the deal? Is she missing a leg? Got a great personality but has a moustache? C'mon...don't con a con, man. I know you're trying to sell me a damaged bit of goods."

Gage laughed but didn't deny it. "So, she's a little on the plump side," he admitted. "But you're always talking about how shallow I am so I figured you'd be willing to take a lovely—albeit *healthy*—lady out for the evening."

"I don't mind a woman with curves," Christian said, shaking his head. "But doing anything that helps you get laid I'm against on principle. I figure I'm saving some woman's heart from getting broken because after you hit it and then don't call her back she's going to cry her eyes out. My foster mother says, 'Karma is a bitch' and, brother, you're headed for a world of hurt very soon the way you've been behaving since I've known you."

"Thank you, Ghandi," Gage retorted with a snort. "Save the morality for when you're back in the sticks of Virginia. This is Manhattan, my friend, where the women are as tough as the men. Besides, when was the last time you enjoyed the company of someone other than your hand?"

Christian scowled. "You're a dick and it's none of your business."

"Be that as it may...you'd be doing me a solid with this one."

"And why do I care about the status of your love life?"

Gage straightened and while a smile remained on his lips, there was something serious there, too. Hell, if Christian didn't know better he'd say that whoever this woman was, Gage was pretty into her for more than just a good time. Christian sighed, hating himself for being a sap. God, his brothers were right, he was a damn romantic at heart no matter how hard he tried to hide it. "Fine," he bit out. "But just dinner and you owe me big-time for this one."

Gage's face broke out into a relieved smile. "You got it."

Christian sighed and left Gage to shower up. While Gage may have hours to spend at the gym, Christian had other commitments.

It was nearing ten in the morning and his stomach was growling but he didn't have time to grab a bite before his next appointment.

He jogged the short steps to the well-kept brownstone and rang the buzzer. A minute later a voice inquired about his business.

"Christian Holt. I'm here to pick up Mathias Breck."

The door buzzed open and he stepped over the threshold as the director of the group home for boys, Sally Hutchins, greeted him with an effusive hug, but there were worry lines bracketing her thin mouth. "Maybe today isn't a good day," she said, causing him to wonder what had happened. They'd had this day scheduled for a month now. He was taking Mathias into the Village for Little League tryouts.

"What's wrong?" Christian asked.

Sally pushed away a lock of fine, graying blond hair and pursed her lips as she shook her head, sadness in her eyes. "I think his visit with his mother didn't go well. He won't talk about it."

"Can I see him?" Christian and Mathias had a lot in common in that they both came from really messed up backgrounds. Christian knew how it felt to sleep with uncertainty, a growling belly and constant fear. Whereas Christian's mother had checked out of this life unexpectedly with an overdose when he was eleven, Mathias's mom was still crashing in and out of the boy's life now and again, most likely when she sobered for a short time, and then disappeared again when her addiction came raging back. It was rough for a kid to see his mom like that. He remembered quite vividly.

Sally closed the door behind him and ushered him into her office, off the main hall. She sighed as she lowered herself into an overstuffed leather office chair. "It was terrible," she shared, drawing Christian into her confidence. "She came and checked him out for the day and everything seemed fine but when he returned—alone—I knew something bad must've happened."

Christian didn't need to ask how a boy managed to navigate the city without an adult. Likely, Mathias had done it often enough at a much younger age, another unfortunate commonality he shared with the young boy. "He didn't tell you what went down?" he asked, curious that Mathias's mother was allowed to check the boy out in the first place.

Sally shook her head. "He buttoned up real quick the minute he walked through the door. Something tells me it was very upsetting."

"Did you file charges against the mother?"

"No, she hasn't broken the law. I did report her to Mathias's social worker, though. Perhaps they can do something about her." She shrugged as if knowing the hope was futile, having seen too many similar scenarios before. "But he's back and that's all that matters, though he's not the same kid. So, I don't know if this is a good idea today."

Christian wasn't deterred. If anything, he was more determined to get Mathias back on track and that included things that kids should be doing, such as Little League tryouts. "Can I give it a try?" he asked.

Sally hesitated, clearly unsure if letting Mathias go with Christian was the right decision, but after another lengthy sigh, she picked up her phone and called for Mathias to come down from the rec room. She pinned Christian with a serious look. "If it looks like he's going to give you trouble, then you bring him right back."

He knew how to handle a kid like Mathias but he gave Sally the assurances she needed so that he could sign the necessary paperwork involved with a day trip.

Ordinarily, anyone not employed by the state wouldn't be able to sign out an unrelated minor housed in the group home but Christian had gone through the mentorship program, which enabled him to work with the kids. He'd gone through extensive background checks that included a full physical workup to ensure that he was suitable to work with the kids housed at the home. It was something he felt strongly about and he didn't mind the hoops he had to jump through as long as he could help some kids out of a rough spot in their lives.

Mathias, a nine-year-old boy with streaks of gold running through his mop, appeared in the doorway, his expression wary until he saw Christian, then a brief light flared in his eyes that spoke of his happiness even if he didn't say a word.

Sally stood and waved Mathias in with a warm smile. "Look who's here to see you...would you like to spend the day with Christian?"

Mathias shrugged. "I guess."

Christian saw through the artful nonchalance

and remembered giving off the same vibe the day he walked through Mama Jo's front door, a bundle of nerves, dread and apprehension beneath a surface of guarded calm. He knew that somewhere in that kid's most private thoughts pulsed a raw wound that Mathias would do anything to protect, including pushing away those who were only trying to help.

"Let's go, buddy," Christian said with a friendly gesture. "Got a full day ahead of us." He waved goodbye to Sally and then they headed out the door.

CHAPTER FOUR

"YOU SHOULD BE RESTING."

Skye ignored the advice. She wasn't about to give up the opportunity to spend some much-needed time with her son to lie around in bed. She slid into her wool coat, taking care not to wince even though the pain nearly took her breath away. It'd been almost two weeks since the beat down so at least her facial bruising had nearly disappeared but her side still hurt like a son of a bitch. She couldn't let on how much it hurt or how much she was suffering or else Belleni's watchdog would make things difficult for her. Once Skye had broken her pinkie toe by accidentally catching the corner of the wall as she ran to help Nico when he'd fallen and even knowing this Vivian had insisted that Skye wear stilettos that night for a client, saying that a former ballerina should be accustomed to pain. Skye forced a smile. "It's a beautiful day and Nico wants to go to the park," she said, adding with enough ice to convey her feelings, "besides, I'm not about to miss my designated day with my son. I see him so little as it is."

"Suit yourself. It matters little enough to me if you're in agony or if you stupidly injure yourself further but Belleni might care if you're unable to fulfill your duties." Vivian Forrone, a woman whose flawless skin yet shrewd gaze made it difficult to determine her true age, pinched her mouth in obvious disapproval as she took in Skye's pallor and mostly faded bruises. She gave the apartment a cursory inspection before saying, "You look like hell. You can't go walking around the city like that." She chided with a scowl, "Belleni said—"

"I don't care what Belleni said," Skye cut in sharply, just saying his name made her want to snarl. It was reckless, acting this way so openly, but she felt the walls closing in and she needed some fresh air before she went crazy. Added to that, she missed her son and felt his absence like a physical ache in her chest and it would take a nuclear bomb going off to stop her from spending time with him today. "I promised Nico and I'm not going to disappoint him."

"*Nico* is not in charge," Vivian reminded Skye with a glint to her icy-blue eyes that almost looked like hatred, and Skye suppressed a wary shudder. Vivian reported to Belleni alone and provided an extra set of eyes on the women that he kept in his stable. Vivian was the equivalent of an office manager/accountant/spy and as far as Skye could tell, the woman relished her job with a zealot's enthusiasm. Skye had often wondered at the relationship between Vivian and Belleni but no one, including herself, had ever had the courage to find the answer. A frown pulled Vivian's smooth brow into disapproving lines.

"We won't be out long," she assured Vivian, moving quickly to get away from her. "Probably only an hour or so."

"Perhaps we should check with Belleni first. I'm sure he'll agree with me that you should stay indoors."

Skye called out to Nico as she headed toward his room. "Vivian, I'm taking my son for some fresh air and I don't care if it snows, we're going out."

Belleni had sent Vivian to help care for Skye while she recuperated but that wasn't the only reason the sharp-eyed woman was suddenly her shadow. Skye wasn't naive; he'd wanted to ensure that Skye knew she still belonged to him by infringing on her privacy.

"This is very unwise," Vivian cautioned, yet her expression was inexpressibly smug, almost glad. "But do as you will. Your star has fallen and it's just a matter of time before it's snuffed out and replaced with something shinier and brighter, someone far prettier than you."

"I look forward to it," she said simply. The day Belleni let her go would be the best damn day of her life, but given their most recent conversation…that wasn't happening anytime soon.

Plainly disappointed by Skye's failure to react more strongly, Vivian switched tracks, aiming for something far more bound to rile her as she queried,

"Have you given any more thought to the Excelsior School for Boys?"

Skye's gaze narrowed. "No. My answer remains the same as it was the first time Belleni suggested it. I want my son to have as normal a childhood as possible and that does not include being sent to boarding school," she said firmly, ignoring Vivian's long exhale of annoyance. Belleni's motivation was transparent enough to Skye. He no longer wanted to be encumbered by a child and shipping Nico off at the earliest opportunity was the easiest answer but there was no way she'd even consider it. Nico was the only thing keeping her sane on some days. "Besides, he's not even old enough to be put on the list so why even talk about it?"

"Oh, please, let's not run in circles about this. I only ask because Belleni is eager to see Nico with an excellent education. Personally, I couldn't care less. But Belleni seems to have taken a mild interest." Her lip curled in distaste and Skye's fingers curled into a tight fist but she made a concentrated effort not to give into her impulse. Punching Vivian would only provide a momentary—albeit deliciously wonderful—satisfaction but it would no doubt create more problems than solve. And she had enough of those on her plate as it was. "Well, I can't expect you to understand the value of a higher education seeing as you barely graduated high school—"

"You know that's not true, Vivian," she interrupted coolly. "I graduated early so I could focus my attention on my ballet."

"Oh, that's right." Vivian made a show of remembering, though Skye knew it was an act. Why they had to play these silly malicious games was beyond Skye but Vivian rarely gave up an opportunity to jab at her. "*Dance.* What a shame that didn't work out, either. Given your experience, I would assume that you would want Nico to focus on getting the best education possible. But what do I know? I'm not a mother."

Thank God for that. She imagined crocodiles were more suited for parenting than the spindle-thin, pointy-jawed, designer-clad menace idly straightening Skye's photos along the mantel. "No, you're not. For everything there is a reason, I suppose," Skye said, not quite able to help herself.

Vivian's gaze cut to hers, frost in her eyes. "Yes, well, not everyone is as *lucky* as you."

Lucky? Skye swallowed the sputter of indignation. She was hardly what she'd consider graced in that area. If anything, ever since she'd booked that flight from Iowa to New York, a black cloud of misery had been hanging over her. Ballet had been her life but if she'd known how cutthroat the professional world of dance was... She suppressed an inward sigh of resignation. Oh, who was she kidding? It wouldn't have mattered. She'd had stars in her eyes and believed stardust in her slippered toes. *Ha.* The old injury twinged in her knee as if to remind her how far she'd fallen from her dreams, pulling her back to the moment and the fact that she was wasting time trading barbs with Vivian when she could be enjoying the day with her son.

"I doubt your services are needed for the rest of the day. Go someplace where you're *wanted*. If there is such a place." Skye allowed a small amount of pleasure at the red creeping up Vivian's neck to stain her cheeks at the insult. "Don't let me keep you from the rest of your day," Skye said, dismissing her as she walked toward her son's room. "I know Belleni keeps you busy with all your responsibilities."

Vivian smiled and grabbed her purse, saying as she opened the door, "Enjoy your day with your son, Skye D'Lane. Perhaps the memory of it will ease your heartache when he's gone. But remember there are eyes in the city. Don't think of running off or else you will find yourself scratched out of Nico's life forever."

The door slammed and Skye flinched. Vivian didn't make idle threats. The woman was a sociopath draped in a socialite's body. Vivian didn't seem to understand or possess anything remotely close to human compassion. She wasn't moved by tears, pleas or heartache. And she seemed to hate children. Or maybe it was just Nico. Another reason Skye wanted Nico out of Belleni's house.

She'd long suspected that Vivian hated her but she'd never figured out why. After she'd become pregnant, she'd realized the true depth of Vivian's aversion as it was reflected in all its purity when she looked at Nico with something between revulsion and fascination. Skye found it extremely unsettling that Belleni had sent Vivian to play nursemaid when there were plenty of other women in his employ who could've fit the criteria.

Nico appeared, a darling angel with a shock of dark hair and deep-set blue eyes the color of diamond-cut sapphires, wearing a hopeful expression that buoyed her as much as it broke her heart that he was being raised in such an environment, and she longed to scoop him into her arms but her protesting rib prevented it. She wiped at her eyes and then pressed a kiss to his forehead. "It's a lovely day, sweetheart. Are you ready for the park?" she asked.

Nico nodded but his gaze went to the door where Vivian had left. "Do I have to go back?" he asked in a small voice. Vivian scared Nico and it renewed Skye's ire that Belleni insisted Vivian be the one to shuttle Nico to the apartment for visits.

"Yes. For now," she answered, wishing things were different. Perhaps, a house will fall on the big, bad witch and at least one half of her misery would disappear. "But she's gone, at least for today," she said with bright cheerfulness. "Ready to have some fun just you and me at the park?"

Nico nodded and smiled up at her, his fears dropping away. "Can we get hot dogs?"

"Of course. A trip to the park isn't complete

without a hot dog with lots of ketchup and mustard, right?"

"Right!"

She carefully wound a warm, woolen scarf around his neck and grabbed his mittens and deliberately pushed aside the knot of fear lodged in her belly for the repercussions that were surely coming for her disrespect. She was going to have a great day with Nico and that's all she was going to think about. Period. "Let's hit it, little man," she announced with a smile. "We've got a whole lot of fun to do before the day is done."

That's right. Fun, damn it.

And she'd mow over anyone who tried to get in their way.

LITTLE LEAGUE TRYOUTS were finished and Mathias and Christian were both starved so they headed for the hot dog vendor that was smart enough to hang around the park during the tryouts. It was there Christian saw her again.

The brisk air had put hearty roses in her cheeks and pinked the tip of her nose but it was the million-watt, sweet smile that stopped him, sucking the air out of his lungs. The memory of her beaten and broken seemed incongruous with the image of her now. Her blond hair, tucked in a messy ponytail trailed down to the middle of her back and she was laughing with a small boy who looked to be around four years old. She wiped mustard from the corners of his mouth while he giggled.

She looked…different. Wholesome. Nothing like the woman he often saw at the bar, waiting, world-weary, jaded.

Her sunglasses hid her eyes but there was no mistaking the love she felt for the boy.

"Are we gonna get some dogs or are you gonna stare at that lady all day?" Mathias asked, annoyed that Christian had simply stopped in his tracks, obviously rattled. Mathias elbowed him. "I'm starved."

He shook himself. "I'm not staring," he denied to the kid who was too street-smart to buy it but Christian couldn't admit that he'd been shocked to see the woman here, in a setting so far removed from where he usually saw her. Looking nothing like she normally did. Not to mention now the worst of the bruising had faded and while she still favored her left side, she looked like a million bucks. He glanced down at Mathias who had shaken his head as if to say "weird" and moved on ahead to get his dog. Christian slowed as he approached the vendor, coming up on her and the boy, and found himself staring harder. Questions better left unanswered crowded his brain and he couldn't look away. Maybe he'd been all wrong about her. The possibility made him feel like an idiot. In this light it was hard to imagine her as the seductress he'd seen. Sure, the worn jeans hugged a near-perfect ass and even though she was layered in warm clothing, he could almost see the outline of firm breasts but there was nothing of the overt siren he was accustomed to seeing.

And hot damn, she was stunning.

CHAPTER FIVE

SKYE FELT EYES ON HER and just as she'd popped her finger in her mouth to suck off the mustard that had dripped from her hot dog, she locked eyes with the man who'd quite literally saved her life.

Sweeps of unruly brown hair ruffled in the breeze curling around the park, the sunlight picking up the subtle golden highlights and accentuating blue eyes that made her think of cool seaside mornings and crisp outdoor days. She pulled her finger from her mouth and looked away. What were the odds in a city crowded with people that she'd run into this man?

"Hey, lady, you're holding up the line," the surly hot dog vendor said, cranky and annoyed. "Keep it movin'. I ain't standing here for my health, you know!"

She risked a short glance at the man again before clasping Nico's hand and walking away with a murmured apology to the vendor.

"Mama? Are you okay?" Nico asked, looking up at her with a frown on his beloved face.

She smiled. "Of course, sweetheart. I was just surprised is all. I thought I knew that man from somewhere but I think I was wrong. C'mon, sweetie, let's find a spot where we can eat these dogs."

Nico seemed content with her answer and quickly forgot as he ate his hot dog. "Mama, I love the park," he announced, a mustard smear on his cheek that she wiped away with her napkin. "Can we come back tomorrow?"

"I don't know…maybe," she hedged, although an unhappy knot twisted her stomach. Belleni refused to keep to a visitation schedule, partly she was sure to keep her tethered and partly because he couldn't be bothered with something he considered so trivial. Never mind that she lived and breathed for the opportunity to spend time with her son. Nico's expression fell and she sighed, giving in. "If it's not raining or snowing, perhaps Belleni wouldn't mind," she said, pleased when Nico grinned. Her son's happiness meant the world to her. She'd risk whatever she had to, to lessen the effects of such an unusual living arrangement for Nico.

"And can we have another hot dog?" he asked.

"Of course," she answered, leaning forward to kiss him on the nose. "Now, eat up, so you can ride the swings."

She kept her smile but on the inside she trembled with a growing sense of urgency to get away from Belleni. Two months ago she'd been on the verge of escape. But that all came crashing down the day Belleni called her to his home.

"Hello, darling," Belleni had said, his voice deceptively mild as she'd entered his sprawling office with its imported Roberto Cavalli rugs and fine-grained, hand-carved mahogany furnishings that cost more than most people saw in a lifetime. At one time she'd been awed by his display of wealth, his obvious fine tastes reflected in the works of art hanging on the walls and the opulence of his home but that was before she'd realized how he consumed lives to pay for his lifestyle. Now it just turned her stomach.

"You wanted to see me?" she asked, nerves stretched thin at the request. At first she'd thought he wanted sex—and though the thought of that man touching her body made her quake with disgust—she'd endure to keep up appearances.

But that wasn't his intent and she should've known when she saw Vivian standing beside him, her eyes aglow with barely concealed glee that something far worse was coming her way.

"Aren't you happy being a Belleni girl?" he asked, throwing her. "Do I not see to your every need?"

"Y-yes," she said, her gaze darting to Vivian, uneasy at the questions he was asking. "Of course. I'm quite happy," she lied.

"I want to believe that, I truly do, but something troubles me," he said with a heavy sigh, his solid body rippling with the motion. He pulled a small slip of paper and gazed at it a long moment, his mouth pursing with displeasure and her blood chilled as she realized what he was staring at.

An ATM slip. Her mind tripped over possibilities.

Had she been sloppy and dropped it somewhere in the apartment? She thought of the last time she visited her bank to make a deposit into her secret account and she held her breath, too afraid to give anything away. That money—painstakingly deposited away from Vivian's watchful eye—was her and Nico's ticket out of this hell. She finally had enough to run. She was just biding her time, looking for the perfect opportunity to slip away....

He let the paper drift from his fingertips in perfect timing as two men Belleni hired as muscle came soundlessly into the room, blocking the exit with their solid mass.

"I took you in off the streets," he began, steepling his fingers as he regarded her with the sharp eyes of the predator he was but she resisted the urge to make a run for it. To run would signify guilt and so far he hadn't actually accused her of anything. "You were such a sad thing when I found you. Full of broken dreams and heartache. I nursed you to health. I gave you purpose. I gave you *Nico*."

"I—"

"Silence!" he interrupted her with a snarl, losing the act of gentle benefactor, shedding it like a snake lost its skin in the heat of summer. "I have nurtured you, cosseted you, protected you...and you repay me with treachery?"

She lifted her chin. "I don't know what you're talking—"

"Stop lying," he demanded, holding her stare for

a long moment as her heart banged painfully against her chest. Did he know how much she'd saved? If so, he knew she'd been planning to bolt. He gestured and the two men advanced on her, grabbing her arms, startling a yelp out of her. He shared a look with Vivian then said, "Here's the situation, my darling. Tomorrow you will go to this bank of yours and you will make a withdrawal..."

Nooo! She struggled against the grip on her arm but they were like steel manacles clamped against her skin and it was no use. Tears sprung to her eyes—born of pain and despair—and began tracking down her cheeks. "I can explain," she began in a desperate bid for damage control but Belleni waved away her attempt.

"You will close your account and the balance will be brought to me as punishment for your deceit."

"It's for Nico," she protested the half truth on a sob, too devastated at the realization that their hope was dead to hold back her tears. She couldn't imagine losing all that she'd saved, not when they were so close. "For his college education. Please...please don't take that from him."

"I want to believe you but I would be a fool. Would you like to know what I think you were going to do?" He continued without her answer. "I believe you were going to use that money to take my son and disappear. After everything I've given you...it's disappointing. Vivian was right—I've given you too much slack. You've forgotten your place. As much as it pains me, it's time to remind you." He looked at the men holding her. "Do not leave too many marks and do not break any bones," he instructed, adding with a sigh. "Nobody pays for a broken Belleni girl, that's for sure." He dismissed them with a wave and Skye was dragged from the room to be taught a lesson in obedience.

"Mama?"

Nico's voice jerked her back to the present and she realized a tear had snaked its way down her cheek without her notice. She lifted her sunglasses and wiped it away. "Sorry, honey. What did you say?" she asked, shaking off the memory with effort. In the past three months she'd endured more than she ever thought possible and that was saying a lot.

"Why are you crying?" he asked in a solemn tone.

She swallowed and regarded him, the love she felt for Nico colliding with the hatred she felt for his father, and she wondered how the hell she was going to get them out of this mess in one piece. "I was just thinking that today is the best day ever and I'll be sad to see it end," she lied, sliding her fingers through Nico's hair and smoothing it away from his face. "But we still have to hit the swings before we call it a day so what do you say? You ready?"

He nodded, but there was still worry in his voice as he said, "Are you sad because of your owies? I have a Band-Aid if you want. They always make me feel better."

A Band-Aid. She bit back the sad laughter and merely smiled at her son's compassion. If only the answer to their problems was so easily found. "You're too sweet for words, kiddo," she said. "But I'm already feeling better so you go ahead and hold on to those Band-Aids for a true emergency. Okay?"

"Okay, Mama," he said dutifully, and then as he clamored to his feet he surprised her with an exuberant, "Race you!" taking off as fast as his sneakered feet would take him in the direction of the swing set.

She sighed, wishing she could chase after him but the painkillers were wearing off and already it was becoming difficult to hide the pain of her ribs. Still, she refused to let anything keep her from enjoying every last moment of the day and climbed to her feet.

Her problems would still be there tomorrow but if Vivian had her way, Nico would not.

CHRISTIAN WATCHED AS SHE followed a small boy, her face alight with joy, and a grin tugged at his lips. Mathias was climbing the monkey bars, swinging like, well, a monkey, and Christian was hard-pressed to keep from staring at the woman as she went to the swings. He had to get her name. He couldn't keep staring at her and referring to her as "the mystery woman" in his mind. He ought to let it go. He already knew she was trouble and he had enough on his plate to heap someone else's problems on it, too. But he had questions. Why'd she leave without even saying goodbye? He figured saving someone's life earned a courtesy chat in the morning. He'd snuck out of a lot of bedrooms in his day but he'd never had a woman sneak from his. But it wasn't about that, not really. He just couldn't get her out of his mind. He wanted to ensure she was all right. He double-checked Mathias and then wandered over to the swing sets.

"I almost didn't recognize you," he said, breaking into a smile that she didn't immediately return. In fact, she seemed quite distressed that he'd approached her, much less addressed her. "You look good," he added, hoping to break the awkwardness between them.

"Thank you," she murmured, returning her attention to the boy he assumed was her son, effectively communicating the "I'm not interested in having this conversation" vibe.

He ought to take the hint but he wasn't ready to walk away just yet. "I just wanted to make sure you were all right. Last time I saw you…" he ventured, hoping she'd take up the lead but he was disappointed.

"Yes, I'm aware of how I looked," she said, ducking his gaze, extreme discomfort radiating from her trim body. "As you can see I'm doing fine. Thank you for your help," she added stiffly.

"I get it. You don't want me in your business. That's coming across loud and clear. Like I said I was just, well, worried. You snuck out before I woke up and I didn't see that coming. I figured we'd at least exchange names or something in the morning. It's not every day I save a woman's life. It was a unique experience and I'm sorry if I don't know how to act."

She had the grace to look ashamed but she also looked panicked that her son might overhear their conversation and for that Christian felt like a jerk. She stepped away from the swing set and he followed. He opened his mouth to apologize but she started first. "I'm sorry. It's not my style to sneak out on someone who's been so kind to me but I'd never been in a situation like that and I didn't know how to act, either." Never? He found it hard to believe that in her line of work she'd never been roughed up before that moment. His mom had been brutalized more times than he could count. Sometimes it'd been a crack across the mouth, other times it'd been broken bones. Maybe that was the difference between a streetwalker and the high-class variety. "Anyway, I'm just here to enjoy the day with my son," she finished with a glance toward the boy on the swings and Christian's gut clenched. Didn't she realize the damage she was doing to her kid by continuing to hook? It didn't matter that she was high-class, she'd still been beaten like a common prostitute. What if she'd died that night? Where would that put her kid?

"It's probably none of my business but you really shouldn't put yourself at risk like you do when you've got a kid depending on you," he said, even though he knew he ought to leave it be.

The wariness returned to her eyes and her mouth firmed as she said coolly, "You're right…it isn't any of your business."

"Fine. But I can tell you that I've seen the damage that parents inflict on their kids because of their choices."

Her mouth twisted. "Speaking from experience?"

"No." Hell yes. But he wasn't about to share the deepest, darkest chapters of his life just to make a point. He gestured at Mathias playing on the playground. "See that boy over there?" he asked.

She followed his subtle gesture then returned to him. "Is he your son?"

"No," he answered, chuckling as Mathias scrambled up the play structure, going up the slide backward instead of using the steps just so he could slide down again. "I'm his designated Buddy." At her frown, he explained, "Mathias is enrolled in a state program for kids at risk. It's like the Big Brother mentoring program but different in that Mathias lives in a group home and I have to sign him out for visits. It's a bit more structured because of the circumstances the kids are in. Circumstances where their parents have put them at risk because of their environment," he added meaningfully.

He expected her to react defensively because that was the standard operating procedure for people when attention was brought to the things that they shouldn't be doing but she surprised him when her hazel eyes warmed. "So you take a kid who is a total stranger out for the day?"

"Yep. Just like renting out a DVD." She drew back and he laughed, saying, "I'm kidding. But yes, I take a kid who is a total stranger out for the day. It helps them to see that not everything is bad out there in the world. Today, I brought Mathias out for Little League tryouts."

"What happens if he makes the team? Does he go to another Buddy?"

"Nope. I signed on for the full season. If he makes the team, I'll pick him up for practices and games. I'll even volunteer on snack day."

"That's quite a commitment," she murmured, but there was a hint of wistful admiration couched in her tone that made him wonder.

He shrugged. "I don't mind. Mathias is a good kid."

"And you do this out of the goodness of your heart?" she asked. "You don't get paid or anything for this?"

"No, I don't get paid but it's worth something to me," he said. Perhaps if he'd had someone to talk to before his mom died, he might've felt less alone, less afraid.

"Oh?"

"I get the chance to make a difference," he answered truthfully. "Not every kid gets an ideal start in life. I'm trying to do what I can to even the score."

Her brow lifted ever so slightly as she said, "If only more people were more like you."

"You don't believe me. I sense sarcasm."

"This is Manhattan. Everyone's got an angle. Yours seems harmless enough, though."

He tried not to take offense. She was right. Everyone did have an agenda but in this, he didn't. However, he wasn't going to waste time justifying himself for it would only make him look guilty. "Believe what you want. Just take me at my word that your actions will affect your son somewhere down the road."

He must've struck a nerve. Her silence felt weighted, filled with something she couldn't talk about without cost. Then he remembered something from that night. "Listen, if you need help…I might be able to hook you up with some resources. I know a lot of people from my connections to the Buddy program."

"You can't help me," she said quietly, shocking him with her bleak honesty. "No one can."

"Are you in some kind of trouble?" he asked. "You mentioned being punished. If you're being forced…" He'd heard of pimps getting dangerously possessive with their girls. He couldn't imagine being under someone's thumb like that. At least with his mother she'd been a free agent. For that small blessing, he'd been grateful. "I could see what I can do."

She gave him a look from her clear hazel eyes that was at the same time hard and vulnerable and he wondered if she realized how much she gave away with that single glance. "I can't afford any more attempts." She drew a halting breath and forced a short smile. "I appreciate your help. I'm sorry I snuck out on you. You deserved better but believe me when I say that I did you a favor."

He didn't doubt her honesty at that moment. And he should've left it at that. She was giving warnings to steer clear of her and her problems. But there was something about her—and it wasn't anything about her physically, which would've been the easy motivation for anyone else—but rather it was when she looked at her son he saw pure love tempered by desolation. He wanted to know why. And he knew full well his curiosity wasn't a good thing but he'd been snagged in the mouth pretty hard and there was no shaking it loose no matter how hard he tried.

"At least tell me your name," he said.

Her groomed brows arched. "What's in a name? The likelihood of ever seeing each other again is slim."

"The odds were slim before today and yet here we are."

"I could give you any name and it wouldn't matter."

"It matters to me."

She held his stare for a long moment and he wondered what went on beyond that careful facade. He suspected a deep well lurked beneath that seemingly still surface. He half expected her to leave him hanging like she did that morning. But she surprised him with an answer. “My name is Skye D’Lane. Thank you…” She paused in question, waiting with a slight tilt of her lips.

“Christian. Christian Holt.”

“Thank you, Christian, for being there.”

SKYE NEARLY BIT HER TONGUE for going against her own decision to remain a mystery. But she’d felt compelled to at least give him her name. She figured it was only fair seeing as he’d saved her life. Yet, as she chewed her bottom lip, she had a strong suspicion a name wouldn’t be enough for a man like Christian Holt. Men like Christian found projects and Skye had just given him the green light to count her among his. A delicate shiver rocked her at the thought.

Perhaps it was the remnant of her distasteful altercation with Vivian that still had her on edge and feeling reckless. Or perhaps it was just that standing there with this incredibly good-looking man who was smiling at her as if she’d just given him the keys to the castle made her feel normal and she hungered for such simple pleasures. “I used to dance,” she said, the need to be anything other than he already knew caused her to loosen her tongue when she otherwise would’ve remained quiet. She never gave up personal information. Her dancing had been her own, a bright, shiny spot on the time line of her life thus far and she protected it with the fierce snarl of a mother bear. And yet, she’d given him this information without a fight.

He eyed her speculatively. "Now when you say dancer…do you mean of the classic variety or the exotic?"

She lifted her chin. "Ballet," she answered with a clip to her tone. She didn't train her entire life, endure countless bruises, bunions, broken toes and forgo anything and everything with too high a calorie count just to swing around on a pole for a few sweaty dollars shoved into her G-string.

"I was going to guess ballet but you never know these days. I've known a few exotic dancers who were pretty talented except your posture gives you away."

"What do you mean? I have excellent posture."

"Exactly. It's too perfect. Ballet dancers have two things in common, seemingly effortless grace and near perfect posture. I knew a girl in high school who dreamed of becoming a ballerina. She practiced endless hours and once told me the way to perfect her form was to pretend she was hanging by a string pulled from the top of her head. I thought it sounded pretty uncomfortable but it must've worked because she was an amazing dancer."

Her cheeks warmed but not in embarrassment, rather with pleasure. To know that was still a part of her, deep down, was a balm to her ragged nerves. "I was good," she said.

"How good?"

"Good enough to land the prima ballerina spot after a year dancing with the New York Ballet."

He smiled, popping a dimple that flirted when his grin deepened. "I'd say that's a fair sight better than just good."

"Perhaps." She laughed in spite of herself. This man was dangerous. Dangerous to someone like her. She had no business engaging in such playful banter, which was exactly why she was enjoying it so much. She glanced at her watch and her good mood started to fade. She called out for Nico to come to her and then returned to Christian with the intention of ending their conversation but before she could, he surprised her again with a request for her phone number.

"I don't think that's a good idea," she said, hesitating.

"Then let me give you mine," he countered, his guileless gaze melting away all the good reasons why she should decline. He pulled a pen from his back pocket and after gently grasping her hand, he flipped her palm and scribbled a set of numbers. "If you want it, it's here. If not, just wash it away."

The skin of her palm tingling from where the pen scrawled, she slowly closed her hand and smiled. "You don't know what's good for you, do you?"

He stepped away, that damnable grin returning. "A character flaw I've never quite been able to root out. Take care, Skye D'Lane."

She watched as he collected the boy he was mentoring and an odd flutter chased her thoughts. What if she'd met someone like Christian instead of Belleni five years ago? How different would her life be today? A painful sigh escaped and she straightened against the longing that served no purpose. Her life wasn't different and there was no place in it for someone like Christian.

And there was no denying how much that sucked.

CHAPTER SIX

"SO YOU LIKE HER OR WHAT?" Mathias asked as they made the trek from the park to the group home. "You got that look on your face that says you want to buy her cable or something."

"Cable, huh? Whatever happened to flowers?"

Mathias shrugged. "Cable takes commitment."

Christian took a minute to mull that one over. "You're right. Never thought about it that way. But I'm not sure I'm ready to take that step. I didn't even get her number."

"She didn't like you?"

"I'm not sure."

"Well, she must've liked you at least a little bit because she talked with you a long time."

"I gave her my number."

Mathias nodded. "You think she's gonna call?"

"I don't know," he answered. "You think she will?"

"Hey, what are you asking me for? I'm just a kid. What do I know about chicks?"

True. "But what does your gut say?" he asked.

Mathias broke into a grin, revealing a jagged front tooth that Christian hadn't noticed before. "She'll call. You're not half-bad-looking for an old dude. If I was a chick I'd give you a ring. If I was old enough. And if I had a phone."

Christian grinned back but privately he was troubled by that tooth. His thoughts immediately centered on how Mathias had received the injury. Was it related to the visit with his mother? The chill in the air was starting to bite. He hadn't meant to stay so long at the park after the tryouts but Mathias had been having a good time, and then he'd seen Skye and all thoughts of returning before the sun disappeared flew out the proverbial window. Now he felt bad. "You cold, buddy?" he asked. "I could give you my sweatshirt."

Mathias waved him away. "Naw, I'm fine. This ain't nothing. Once my ma passed out and accidentally locked me outside and it was snowing."

"That's rough. How'd you get back in your place?" he asked, keeping his tone casual.

"Easy, I just climbed the fire escape and slipped in through the neighbor's window. Freaked 'em out when they saw me run through their living room, though," he said, laughing at the memory.

"That happen a lot?"

"What do you think? I'm in a group home. They don't put kids in places like that 'cause they're living like Disney."

"It's not so bad, is it? Living at the group home with Ms. Hutchins?" he asked.

Mathias kicked at a pebble on the split sidewalk

and watched as it clattered down the way until it hit a trash can with a loud clink. "It's okay, I guess. Better than most. Better than the last that's for sure," he muttered, mostly to himself. "But it still sucks to live with a bunch of strangers with no privacy and stuff."

"Yeah, I remember what that's like," he shared, nodding. He'd spent a year bouncing from one foster home to another before he landed with Mama Jo. And some of those homes were downright criminal. There were too many people in the foster care system who were in it purely for the money…or worse. "So, how'd the visit with your mom go? Ms. Hutchins said you won't talk about it. What happened?"

"Nothing," Mathias said too quickly and with a short scowl, hunching his shoulders ever so slightly as if trying to make himself disappear. Damn, Christian recognized that posture, too.

"Same kind of nothing that broke your tooth?" he asked, keeping his gaze focused straight ahead, not breaking stride. "Was it your mom?"

"No."

"A boyfriend?" When Mathias remained silent Christian knew the answer. He bit back a hard curse word. "Are you okay?" he asked.

"Yeah," Mathias answered, his young voice struggling to sound flippant but instead to Christian's ears sounded thin and small. Someone had kicked this kid around. It was no wonder he split, choosing a group home he hated over home. "It's no big deal."

"You got any other bruises?" When Mathias shook his head, Christian braced himself for the answer to his next question. "Has your mom's boyfriend hurt you anywhere else?" God, what a shitty thing to have to ask a kid but he had to know.

"He ain't jacking me if that's what you're getting at," Mathias said but there was a tremor of fear hiding under the anger. What Christian heard was, "maybe." Or "if not yet, soon." He wanted to snarl at someone. He'd have to say something to Sally about his suspicion. Mathias looked up at Christian, his tongue snaking out to touch the jagged tooth. "Is it real noticeable?" he asked.

"A bit. That's why you haven't been talking to anyone, isn't it?"

Mathias glanced away. "Yeah."

"It needs to get fixed. The state will pay for a trip to the dentist."

"Yeah, but they'll cover it with that silver stuff or something and I'll look like a hood rat. I'd rather just leave it the way it is. It's not as sharp as it was."

"How about this…let me talk to Ms. Hutchins. I'll make sure you don't get that silver amalgam."

Mathias eyed him with suspicion, plainly not accustomed to someone doing something for him or keeping their word about it. "How?"

"Let me worry about that. Just promise me you'll talk to Ms. Hutchins about what happened."

"I don't know," Mathias said, unsure.

"Look, I know you're trying to protect your mom.

But you gotta look out for you, too. Your mom—if she was thinking straight—would want you to be safe, right?"

Mathias nodded, then looked away but not before Christian saw the shine in his eyes. Yeah, he remembered how it felt to be sandwiched between loyalty and fear, unsure of who to trust and totally clueless as to how to change the circumstances. What Christian knew now that he didn't know then was no kid had the power to change their parents, no matter how much they loved them. He had Mama Jo to thank for that revelation.

They came up on the brownstone just as the last of the day's milky sunlight gave way to darkness. The streetlamps popped on but the light didn't reach far. Sally opened the door, exasperation pursing her lips as she ushered the boy inside. "Cutting it a bit close, don't you think?" she admonished, prompting a sincere apology on his part. Sally forgave him quickly, though, when she saw a difference in Mathias. "Go upstairs and get cleaned up, Mathias. Dinner is waiting. I'll just be a few minutes with Christian."

Sally waited for Mathias to disappear upstairs for a quick scrub and then turned to Christian, her sharp gaze missing nothing. "What did he tell you?" she asked.

"The mom's boyfriend broke his front tooth," he began and when Sally gasped, he continued with grim certainty. "And my gut instinct tells me the guy is more than just physically abusive. Mathias said he hasn't touched him but…I'm not sure. Maybe you could check into it?"

"Absolutely," Sally said, her mouth softening with concern for her young charge. That's what Mathias loved about Sally. She cared. She didn't look at the boys in her care as just another dollar sign. Each line in her face was put there from the countless smiles she gave to each kid. Christian knew people like Sally were a rarity, like Mama Jo. "Thank you, Christian. For being there for Mathias," she said softly, causing Christian to shift in his shoes.

"I don't mind. He's a good kid," he said, moving to the door.

"Yes, he is. But he's lucky to have you on his side."

Christian smiled around his own memories crowding him. "No, I think I'm the lucky one," he said. Christian knew the difference a positive influence made on a kid teetering on the edge of despair and ruin. "So, listen, Mathias is worried that the dentist will use the silver amalgam for his tooth. I want to pay for the repair myself. Make sure the dentist matches his teeth perfectly. I don't want the kid to have one more thing to worry about, you know?"

Sally smiled kindly. "You're a sweetheart. I will find out how much it will cost and then you can make a donation to the home. I will see to it that the money is used for his dentistry. Bless you, Christian."

Yeah…well, he didn't know about that but it felt good to do something for the kid. Even if it was just a tooth.

SKYE HAD ONLY JUST TUCKED NICO into bed when she heard her apartment door open. Her mouth tightened as a rush of impotent anger followed. She had no control over who came and went in her own home because it belonged to Belleni. And likely, it was either Belleni or Vivian who had arrived unannounced and *uninvited.*

She closed Nico's door with a gentle click and braced herself for whatever was coming next.

As expected, Belleni was in her living room, making himself comfortable on her sofa. Although a smile wreathed his lips, his eyes were calculating, shrewd.

"Can I get you something to drink?" she asked, nearly gagging on the false hospitality. How many times had she imagined watching him fall dead to the floor? In the past year, too many to count. But the man was irritatingly healthy and not likely to oblige her with a nicely timed heart attack any time soon. She went to the bar and pulled his favorite brandy.

He accepted the snifter with a faint smile. "It's nice to see you haven't forgotten all your manners, darling," he said, sipping at the Mendis coconut brandy that cost more than a thousand dollars a bottle. She never touched the stuff but Belleni insisted that all his top girls, as in the women he housed personally, keep it in stock just for him. "Now tell me why you persist on being difficult? Vivian tells me you have been exceedingly rude and petulant, particularly when it comes to Nico."

Her breath hitched in her throat but she revealed nothing. To show fear was to give him an added advantage. There was precious little she could control except herself so she clung to it like a bull terrier. "Vivian and I had a disagreement. Nothing more, nothing less," she said with a shrug. "And as it turned out, everything was fine. The weather was beautiful and we had a great day at the park."

"She said you are adamant that Nico will not attend Excelsior."

"He's four. He's too young to even talk about it," she said evasively, moving to sit as far from him as possible but he thwarted her intention by purposefully patting the cushion beside him. Her heart thudded painfully but she didn't disobey. Marinating in the revulsion she felt now, it was hard to remember a time when she'd thought he was the kindest, most amazing man she'd ever met. When she'd been vulnerable and lost, he'd appeared like a guardian angel, showering her with gentle affection, expensive gifts and wooing her with promises that he never planned to keep. She swallowed the lump that had risen but she forced a smile, which seemed to appease him a bit. "Belleni, I know you want the best for Nico but he needs me right now. There will be plenty of time to consider the possibility of a private boarding school when he's of age to attend. Right now, with everything…I think he needs stability."

"Perhaps," he mused, but she could tell he wasn't really listening. He was toying with her. "Or perhaps it would do you both some good to be apart for a while…"

"We're already kept apart," she reminded him tightly. "Don't you think you've punished me enough by keeping him from me?"

"A son should be with his father," Belleni remarked absently, more interested in her breasts than the topic of conversation but she wasn't about to let it slide.

"Nico doesn't even know you're his father," she said in a low tone so as not to disturb Nico. "To him you're a stranger who just happens to live in the same house. And Vivian…" She could barely manage the woman's name without revealing her hostility. "She terrorizes him with impunity. You do nothing to stop her from hurting him and at the very least you ought to protect him because he's your only flesh and blood."

Belleni's stare narrowed at her impassioned statement and she knew she'd pushed too hard. "Perhaps Nico should not stay here tonight. You seem overwrought," he said harshly. "Vivian is right, you should be resting."

No! She slid her tongue across lips that had gone numb and fought the rising panic that Belleni might force her to rouse Nico from his dreams to drag him crying back to that house where he went to sleep afraid each night because Vivian refused to allow the boy a nightlight in spite of the fact that he was terrified of the dark. She told Skye a boy with Belleni's blood should fear nothing, least of all a few shadows. Then she'd accused Skye of coddling him.

"I misspoke," she whispered, choking down what she really wanted to say which was that she wished with the power of a thousand suns that Belleni would die a miserable death alone and afraid so that he could reap all the misery he'd sown his entire life. Tears pricked her eyes and she tried to hide it but Belleni sensed her pain and drank it like ambrosia. His finger caught her chin and pulled her to him. "Please, Belleni, don't take my son from me. He's so little...he needs me," she heard herself plead, hating his power over her.

He smiled, true pleasure reflecting in his eyes. His gaze traveled the planes of her face as hunger gathered in his cold stare. "*I* need you, my darling," he murmured, sliding his finger down her neck to the valley of her breasts. "You intoxicate me. Even pregnancy did not dull your beauty. In fact, you bloomed like a winter rose in a hothouse garden whereas most wither and become ugly. Your body is still ripe and your breasts are still lush and firm," he said, his breathing quickening, nauseating her, as his hand reached over to cup and knead the flesh through her shirt. *Don't touch me. I hate you.* She closed her eyes against the feel of his hands on her body. His touch became impatient as he withdrew and gestured for her to undress. "It's time we get reacquainted, my love," he said, beginning to unbuckle his pants.

"I—I can't," she stammered, surprising him with

her refusal. She knew if he touched her again she'd scream. "The doctor said I can't have any physical activity until my rib heals or…I could be down for another few weeks."

She drew faint satisfaction in watching his lust fade as his business sense took over. He grunted his displeasure but righted his pants with a glower. "I will see that pig who did this to you punished beyond his worst nightmare. Vincent gave him but a taste of what will happen next," he promised, though she held no illusions he was making a grand gesture on her part. He was angry at being denied and he needed an outlet.

She nodded and smiled her relief, which was genuine. "Thank you, Belleni," she murmured, her voice shaking a little as the adrenaline drained from her body. It was only a brief reprieve, she knew, but it was something. Belleni went through periods where he couldn't get enough of her and then he would abandon her and put her back in the stable, almost as if he were punishing her for his obsession. It would seem his desire for her and her alone had returned, and she would only be able to put him off for so long. But she'd take the short respite wherever she could find it.

He climbed to his feet, adjusting his clothes with short, clipped movements, betraying his simmering agitation. "This fighting between you and Vivian must stop," he advised her sternly. "I don't have time to referee your silly arguments."

"She hates Nico," Skye said, unable to hold her tongue. "Nothing she says comes from a pure place in her heart. How am I supposed to trust her around him?"

Belleni was silent for a moment, then said with something that almost sounded like regret and she couldn't help but stare. "It is difficult for her…the child. I will speak with her," he added with a sigh. "But in the meantime, do not borrow trouble."

She murmured something appropriately dutiful yet she was the farthest from compliant in her mind. She felt the pressure of time weighing on her. Her escape route had been effectively cut off and as soon as Belleni felt she was well enough for sex, he'd return. Or he'd take Nico from her. She felt the threat hovering in the air, filling the corners with malice even if he hadn't actually uttered the words. She knew how he operated. Belleni took what mattered most in the world for leverage. And Belleni knew nothing mattered more to her than her precious boy.

As if sensing the direction of her thoughts, he smiled and said, "Bring the boy back to me tomorrow."

She gritted her teeth but nodded. "Of course."

Approval gleamed in his stare but he wasn't quite finished. He cocked his head at her. "Aren't you going to kiss me good-night, perhaps thank me for my generosity?" She swallowed the bile that rose and pasted a benign smile on her lips. As she crossed to him, he pulled her in tight, until her breasts rubbed against

CHAPTER SEVEN

CHRISTIAN KEPT ROLLING Skye's name on his tongue from the time he returned Mathias to the group home and entered his loft.

Skye…what a perfect name for her, he mused until he realized with a start that he was beginning to think a little too much about her. He wanted to help her but he couldn't start thinking of anything else with her. She was a fine woman, no doubt, hell, a woman like her went beyond the term "trophy wife" if she were of a mind to walk away from the sordid business that was her life but, the fact remained that he'd never be able to look beyond the actions of her past. At least he was straight up about it, he thought. Other men might string her along for the sex and the pleasure of her company until they tired of the game. He'd never do that to her. He'd never do that to anyone but he knew men who did and would.

She hadn't called. He wasn't surprised. He went to his computer and searched her name on Google just to see what popped up. He found a few playbills with her name and a picture or two of her dressed in her tutu. She had that rare quality that seemed to blossom with maturity rather than fade. He clicked on an old bio and read it with interest. Small town girl moved to the big city when she was only eighteen, made prima ballerina at nineteen and her career was over by twenty. He drew back, a furrow in his forehead. Man, that must've sucked. By the looks of it her star had shot into the sky only to plummet a short time later. He imagined that had to sting even to this day. Making a living in the arts was a tough gig. He knew the odds were against most people from the moment they started. Still, he wished Skye's story had ended differently.

He clicked past a few more links and found an agent contact for the ballerina Skye D'Lane. He drew back in his chair, cocking his head in thought. What if the agent still had a number for her? The chances were beyond slim but hey, weirder things had happened lately. He grabbed his cell and dialed the number.

"Barry Friedman," the guy on the other line said in a distinctive New Yorker accent.

"My name is Christian Holt. You don't know me but I'm looking for a former client of yours, Skye D'Lane."

"She's out of the business," he replied, sounding disinterested in furthering the conversation. "I heard she moved back to the cornfields of Idaho or Iowa. Something like that."

"Do you have a contact number for her?"

"Surely you know she's been out of the scene for the past five years?"

"I know. Do you have a contact number or not?" he asked, irritated at the guy's dismissive tone.

He sighed on the other line. "So pushy." The sound of papers shuffling, and then he returned, saying, "You're in luck. I have a number. Now, what do you want her number for?"

"I'm a huge fan," he answered.

"Not a stalker I hope."

"No, not at all."

"Well, she's not my client so I'm no longer bound by client confidentiality. Here, knock yourself out." He rattled off the number and Christian jotted it down. "Listen, if you see her, tell her no hard feelings. Some things just aren't meant to be."

"Yeah sure." Barry Friedman was a fount of empathy and compassion. "Thanks," he said, and hung up, eager to get off the phone. Staring at the number he wondered if he ought to call her. It was one thing to acquire the means, quite another to actually put something into motion.

Tomorrow, he decided. He'd call tomorrow afternoon before his shift started at the bar. But what would he say? He didn't know. He needed strategy. But he hardly knew her so what could he use…a slow grin spread across his face as an idea came to him.

But first, he needed to call someone else. If everything worked out, by tomorrow he'd have his in.

SKYE COULDN'T SLEEP. She flopped onto her stomach and bunched her pillow beneath her but she might as well be lying on rocks for all the comfort she was getting. Her thoughts were a ridiculous mess. She had Belleni to thank for that, she grumbled to herself but even as she thought it, she knew that wasn't entirely true. Of course, he was in her head but something—or someone—was also taking up space in her thoughts and frankly, it shocked her.

Christian.

A total stranger. A man she should definitely steer clear of. She didn't need nor want another complication in her life. Yet, he kept popping up in her head, teasing her with that boyish dimple and those ridiculously blue eyes.

For just a wild, reckless moment she wondered what it would be like to enjoy a little harmless flirtation. To allow herself the freedom to engage in playful banter that wasn't a means to an end, an act she put on to charm the client. She wondered what it'd be like to go on a date with someone who didn't have the expectation of sex just because he paid a little extra for her services. She wanted to remember what it felt like to go to dinner with someone and as they sat apart from one another, be just as ignorant of how the evening was going to play out as the other person. Would they kiss? Would they hold hands? Would they want to see each other again? It'd been so long since she'd enjoyed such simple dating rituals that she almost didn't remember how they worked.

She allowed her thoughts to wander further, tantalized by the engaging fantasy of mundane normalcy, to wonder where Christian took a woman on a first date. Was he the kind of guy who did the dinner and flowers thing or was he the adrenaline junkie type who took a date bungee jumping? She hoped he was somewhere in between.

She smiled at the memory of how persistent he'd been at the park, the way his eyes had lit up for a boy that wasn't related to him but still gave him joy. She allowed a small sigh. What would it be like to be with someone so generous? She turned on her back and stared at the ceiling. Once she'd thought Belleni was kind. But what she'd mistaken for kindness had actually been a calculated facade. How had she ever been so naive?

Ten thousand dollars. Gone. Handed over to Belleni as punishment for her deception. It curdled her stomach to think of how close she'd been to putting this whole sordid mess behind her only to fail so miserably. If only Belleni would find someone else to fulfill his obsession. She didn't understand why he remained fixated on her. By all accounts she was difficult to manage, needed constant supervision and had already tried to run several times with disastrous results. Yet, he continued to tether her to his side like an exotic collared pet. And God, how she chafed at his possession.

If it weren't for Nico she'd have found a way to split a long time ago. But her son was Belleni's ace and he played it whenever he felt the need to corral her. He parceled out visitations like tiny morsels to a starving person. He threatened to send Nico away to his family in Italy if she didn't behave. The boy already had dual citizenship due to his father and it would be easy to spirit the child out of the country with Belleni's influence. That's why she'd banked up the ten grand, to ensure they left no trace of their disappearance and could stay underground for at least a year in the hopes of leaving Belleni behind forever. A mere couple thousand wouldn't have sustained them long enough. But it was all gone now.

She supposed this was another of those little reminders that Belleni had all the power and she had none. She would get through it. And she would find another way out of this craptastic mess.

She just needed more time.

And a miracle.

BELLENI STROKED HIS NEATLY groomed facial hair, his thoughts troubled. Vivian, his right-hand man, so to speak, was talking about something he should care about but his focus was elsewhere. He felt the years pressing on him like never before. He suspected it had something to do with the recent turn of events surrounding Skye and her deception. Somehow she'd managed to amass a tidy sum of money without his knowledge, squirreling it away for more than a rainy day. He ached at the knowledge that she'd been planning to run. Had he not given her every advantage? Provided her with a life most would covet? He asked so little of her but expected her loyalty. His hand stilled, dropping to his side to clench in anger. Had he not rescued her from despair when she'd lost everything dear to her? Did he not allow her to contact her family once a year? It was more than he allowed his other girls. And yet…she repaid him with treachery. She was a jewel in his crown but he swore she was poison, too.

"Your melancholy is obvious." Vivian cut into his thoughts, pulling his attention with her sharp tone. She arched a thin brow, adding with a put-out sigh, "As is the cause. What are you going to do with her?"

"What's to do? There is nothing to do," he groused, irritated that Vivian knew him so well but that was to be expected given all that they'd shared over the years. He roused himself to broach a subject he knew was bound to ruffle feathers but there was no avoiding it. "Vivian, you must stop being so harsh to Nico. It upsets Skye."

"Oh, does it? And why should I care if a whore is upset?" she asked, blinking in feigned surprise.

"Don't play innocent. It is beneath you."

Her face hardened. She regarded him with those chilly blue eyes, saying, "Fine. This ridiculous obsession of yours with that woman is going to destroy all you've built. Let her go. It's beside the time to do so. There are hundreds of girls out there who will suit the same purpose with less trouble. I say good riddance."

He couldn't say the same. He couldn't let her go.

It gave him a physical pain that baffled him. And it drove him to madness to think of her building a life away from him. "She is a moneymaker," he stated as if that were the only reason he refused to cut her loose. Though, he knew in his heart of hearts, Vivian spoke the truth. He was crazy to keep her around. She was a loose cannon. Or worse, a ticking time bomb. "She has grace, class and style aside from physical beauty. Besides, I have invested too much to simply make her disappear now."

"Yes, we all know how you've made a fool of yourself," she said, her tone clipped and disapproving. He cast a short look of warning her way but she ignored it. "You've created an additional challenge with that boy. I can only imagine what you were thinking. He is more than a loose end. He is a liability. An unfortunate accident is your only way out of this growing mess of a situation."

"Stop talking nonsense, woman," he barked, annoyed that she would even suggest such a thing. "He is my son. You seem to have forgotten that important fact."

Her mouth pinched and her body tightened in a rigid line. In that moment he could've sworn hatred flared in her eyes and he wondered if perhaps the ghosts from the past were becoming too much for her. The moment dragged out between them and guilt prodded at him to offer a gentle word but she collected herself to say, "It is impossible to forget. He is your spitting image."

That he was. And it gave him an odd thrill that Skye's child shared his genes. If only she didn't loathe him. Oh, yes, he knew. A heavy weight settled on his shoulders, pushing him further into a sorry state of mind. He wished it didn't matter, that she was like so many of the others, but there was something about her that pushed him to do things he'd never consider with anyone else.

Such as father a child.

He averted his stare away from Vivian, away from the condemnation radiating from her thin frame. "You will stop this nonsense when it concerns Nico," he demanded roughly, risking a look at the woman who knew all his secrets. "He is my family. Like it or not."

She inclined her head in his direction, her rage cooling into a bitter freeze. "Of course. Then, I would suggest you exert your influence on Skye and convince her to send him away. She will poison him against you eventually. Mark my words. She will ruin you through that boy," she counseled. "Besides, allowing her to have Nico around makes her difficult to manage."

He grunted his agreement. Vivian had a point. And he sensed that Skye would endeavor to find another way to bolt. But he knew she would stay put if he held her son, which is why he refused to return him to her full-time. "Excelsior is a fine school," he mused, catching a quiet gleam of triumph in Vivian's eyes. "And a boy such as Nico will need the best education there is. Procure the necessary arrangements to ensure his early enrollment."

For once Vivian's smile reached her eyes but it was enough to chill his blood. "It would be my pleasure," she murmured, exiting the room with a soft chuckle.

He stared after Vivian, wondering when the woman had become so cold, so vicious.

Of course, he didn't need to wonder long. He already knew the answer.

It was the day he'd made her abort their child… twenty years ago.

Perhaps that was the weight he felt. Suddenly, he felt each of his fifty-two years as if they were bricks of cement pressing on his body.

Their child would've been an adult by now. He sighed. Funny how life had its twists and turns. He hadn't wanted to be a father to Vivian's child and truly, when Skye had told him she was pregnant, he hadn't been pleased. Until he realized it was the perfect way to tie her to him forever. Then, the prospect of fatherhood had improved.

And he'd been correct. The child was better leverage than he could've dreamed.

With the boy firmly in his control, he had Skye caged like a little bird.

Just the way he liked her.

He smiled and made a mental note to give Vivian a little bump in her salary. The woman deserved a little extra. It was the least he could do.

CHAPTER EIGHT

SKYE WAS JUST BUNDLING Nico into his jacket and mittens when her cell rang. She glanced at the number, tempted to let it go to voice mail when she didn't recognize the number but sheer curiosity got the better of her. She answered and Christian's smooth voice caused goose bumps to riot along her forearms as a reluctant smile followed.

"Before you think that I'm calling you up just to chase you around for a date, I have a proposition for you that is entirely altruistic," he said.

"How did you get my number?" she asked, puzzled but secretly impressed.

"The internet is a wondrous thing," he said by way of an answer but continued to his original statement. "Are you interested?"

"What kind of proposition would that be?" she asked, wary but admittedly, intrigued. She couldn't remember the last time someone asked her for something without ulterior motives.

"Well, you know the program I was telling you about? The Buddy program has an affiliate program for girls called My Big Sister and they're looking for someone to come in a few times a week to start the arts classes with the kids. And of course, I thought of you."

"Me?" she asked, mildly distressed yet flattered at the same time. "Why me?"

"Why not? You're a classically trained dancer and that falls under the arts, doesn't it? Besides, I read somewhere that dance can help kids focus and gives them a good introduction to new opportunities." He must've sensed her reluctance because he pressed a bit harder, his earnest tone pulling at her. "I don't know what your childhood was like but I can tell that these kids don't come from the best. At the least they've suffered neglect but at the worst…well, some have forgotten that there's anything beautiful left in the world. The arts help to remind them what's out there."

How could she argue with that? Everything he said was true. You could tell a story with dance. At her best, she'd been able to paint a picture with the sweep and twist of her arms and body, forgetting everything else going on in her life, good or bad. She missed it so much it was a constant ache but she'd written off any chance of ever dancing again. Tears pricked her eyes at even the thought of sliding her toes into ballet slippers again. Dance was something that had been wholly her own, something Belleni had never touched. "I'll do it," she blurted before she could change her mind or, worse, plain come to her senses. Belleni would disapprove but she didn't care. "I would love to teach the children about dance.

When and where?" she asked, a bit breathless, yet smiling.

She could hear the smile in his voice as he said, "I was hoping you'd say that. How about I swing by and pick you up Friday around noon?"

"How about you give me the address and I'll meet you there?" she countered.

He laughed. "All right," he conceded with good humor. Another point in his favor. He gave an address on the west side of Central Park and she quickly entered it into her phone. "See you Friday, then."

"Friday," she agreed, and added, "Thanks for thinking of me, Christian."

"It's all I've done since we met," he answered, his honest answer chasing a thrill down her spine like kittens after a ball of string. "I want to help you."

"I'm not a project for you to fix, Christian," she said, the intoxicating warmth curling in her belly cooling considerably. "And I don't need your pity."

"And I'm not offering it. But I am offering you something that I think you'll enjoy."

A bit unsettled but not quite sure she was capable of refusing, her desire to dance blotting out any sensible argument against accepting, she agreed to meet with him.

Butterflies erupted and joined in her stomach with a vague sense of unease for her recklessness but the lure was too strong. She'd have to lie to Vivian about her whereabouts but she'd do anything to be able to forget for just a moment where her life had stalled and left her stranded.

Just one moment. She huffed a shaky breath.

She'd sort out her feelings later. After her meeting with Belleni.

"I DON'T LIKE IT HERE. I want to stay with you, Mama," Nico said, pressing against her side. She understood her son's distaste. For it's obvious wealth, it had nothing in the way of warmth. It was all designer, imported, ostentatious presentation. Belleni did that on purpose. Belleni had once confided to her that wealth put on display was a quick way to impress without saying a word. It said the company of a Belleni girl didn't come cheap and that only those within a certain tax bracket need apply. It was hard to remember a time when she'd been impressed with the obscene showing. She seemed a shadow of that corn-fed, naive girl who'd stepped off the bus and onto the city streets so long ago.

Vivian, with her hateful blue eyes, greeted them in the foyer and ushered them not into the study where Skye expected the meeting to take place but rather into the living room.

"Mama, take me back to our apartment," Nico said fretfully, to which Vivian flashed a disdainful look before giving a minute shake of her head.

"Hush, sweetie," Skye said, but gave his small hand a reassuring squeeze to communicate that she understood. She didn't like this place, either.

Vivian opened the double doors and watched as they entered. Belleni sat in a large, overstuffed fine leather chair that looked softer than butter and likely cost an exorbitant amount. His mouth lifted in an inviting smile but Skye was immediately put on guard by the shrewd light in his eyes. She glanced at Vivian and was further alarmed by the gleam in her eyes. Anything that excited Vivian usually bode terribly for Skye. Their earlier conversation came back to haunt her and she swallowed in trepidation.

"Take a seat, my darlings," Belleni instructed, then turned to Nico. "Would you like a root beer float?" he asked Nico. When her son nodded shyly, he gestured to Vivian who stepped forward with an outstretched hand to Nico.

"Come, boy," Vivian said, trying to sound kind, which to Skye's ears was downright terrifying. She started to protest but Vivian had already clamped her hand around her son's, pulling him to his feet and out the door before Skye could stop her.

"What's this about, Belleni?" Skye asked, unable to stand the tension stringing her taut. Her gaze strayed to the door where they'd exited and she was half tempted to run after the woman. "I'm uncomfortable with Nico being with her. I told you she doesn't like him."

Belleni waved away her concern. "I've already taken care of that. Vivian has seen the error of her ways and is looking to make amends."

"She's lying," she said, bordering on panic. "She

hates him and is only waiting for the right opportunity. The last time she brought him to me he had finger bruises on his arms. Children are fragile, Belleni. Promise me you'll protect him."

"Silence," he demanded, his eyes flashing. "I told you I took care of the situation and unlike you who has a penchant for questioning my decisions, others do not. Vivian will do as I tell her. Now behave yourself before I truly lose my temper with you."

She blinked back tears, fighting an awful sense of foreboding yet she held her tongue and waited.

"It's like this…the time has come for me to bring Nico into his rightful place."

Her blood chilled but she remained calm. "What does that mean?"

"Don't pretend stupidity," he said. "Nico is my son and someday he will inherit my legacy."

She paled at the thought of Belleni inducting Nico into his den of iniquity. She was still reeling from Belleni's discovery of her cache of money. But she had thought she'd have more time to recover before Belleni started pushing for some kind of true relationship with their son. She'd never wanted Nico to know his true roots. *Never.* "Why now?" she asked. "You haven't treated Nico with anything aside from passing interest up until now. He doesn't even understand you're his father."

"Yes, well, that will change," he said sharply.

"You're doing this to punish me, aren't you?" she asked, her chest so tight she could barely get air into her lungs. "It's because you're angry with me over my disagreement with Vivian, well, I take it back. I'll do whatever she likes from now on."

He sighed. "It pains me that you would think so low of me that I would use my own child to get back at you over some tiff with Vivian. Please, darling," he said, his tone aggravatingly patronizing.

She settled herself, forcing calm into her voice. "Then what is it?"

His gaze narrowed. "The boy distracts you. And it is time to refocus."

"Refocus on what?" she asked, the edge returning to her voice even as she tried to school it into civility. "You've taken everything from me, you'd take my son, too?"

"Don't be so melodramatic. Your son will remain your son. You're the one who has caused this turmoil in your life. If I could trust that you wouldn't run away I wouldn't have had to take such drastic measures by keeping Nico with me. Perhaps you should spend more time trying to find a way to be less deceitful and more trustworthy and then we could discuss a new arrangement. As it stands, I cannot trust that you won't take my son and disappear at your first opportunity. Truly, Skye, it wounds me that you are so ungrateful."

She swallowed. For one wild moment she longed to threaten to call the police, to spill every dirty detail she'd managed to glean since knowing Belleni but he held too many cards and he knew it. She also longed to curl her hands into fists. She imagined pummeling his rotten face until she could no longer make out his features but that wasn't an option. He was too powerful, too connected and she wasn't going to prison over him.

"Vivian thinks it would be good to start Nico's education early at Excelsior," he said. "It would seem you've become too attached and in truth, it's not good for a boy to become too close to his mother. A little distance would do you both some good."

"Don't send him away," she said, tears not far from her voice. "Please."

"Vivian says—"

"Vivian is not his mother. I am," she cut in softly. "Am I not a good mother to your son?"

"There is room for improvement, such as when you coddle him too much, but overall, you are a good mother," he agreed.

"Then, trust me," she said, hating that he could compel her to beg but the idea of sending Nico away to some school thousands of miles away made her insane. She swallowed bile as she said, "I'll try harder to be a good girl. I won't try to run. I promise. I'm happy here."

"I've heard this before," Belleni groused, but she could tell he was softening a bit. "You tell me what I want to hear, that is all."

"I know you want the best for Nico," she said, lying through her teeth and nearly choking on each word as they passed her lips. "Can you blame me for being protective of our son? I would die if something happened to him."

Belleni cast a look her way as if gauging whether or not she'd just given him a warning but he seemed weary of fighting for the moment. He waved her off, irritation in his expression as he said, "We will address this again later. My head aches and my gut is cramping. But, Skye," he said, his stare narrowing, "soon your services will be required and I will not accept any excuses so use your time to rest. Now go."

SKYE WOULD RATHER DRINK Drano than let Belleni touch her but he had that glint in his eye again, the one that told her he wanted her and no other. Time was running out.

The switch had been flipped and there was no going back. Once she'd been biding her time as she banked money on the side but now that that was destroyed, she had to find plan B and fast.

Vivian appeared in the foyer as she was leaving. "You think you've won this round, don't you?" she asked.

"I'm sure I don't know what you mean," Skye retorted, moving toward the door, but Vivian prevented her from leaving by slapping the flat of her palm against the door. Skye regarded her coolly. "Please remove your hand."

"This isn't over…not by a long shot," Vivian warned, her gaze boring into Skye's. "You're nothing but a whore whose only currency lies between her legs but even that will eventually lose its appeal and you'll no longer have any leverage."

"Vivian, if you hate me so much…why don't you exert that considerable influence on Belleni and convince him to send me and Nico packing? I would gladly take my son and go."

Vivian withdrew her hand. "You think I haven't?" she asked, surprising Skye with her simple question. "But it doesn't matter. What Belleni wants, he gets. And for the time being, he seems to want you. It's a mystery I've tired of trying to unravel. It's a waste of energy. Besides, this obsession can't last forever."

One can hope. But something told her Belleni would never let her go. And that's what scared her. "Vivian, we don't have to be enemies," she said.

At that Vivian's mouth turned up in a smirk that was almost sad around the edges as she said, "No? Well, we sure as hell can't be friends, so what does that leave?"

"Something in between? Two people with the same goal," Skye offered, taking a chance on the glimmer of banked emotion in Vivian's eyes. She didn't know Vivian's story but she suspected there was pain buried beneath those layers of ice. And she also suspected Belleni was at the root. Imagine that, the broker of emotional agony being at the epicenter of someone else's tragedy. "I want to leave and you want me gone. We don't have to be friends…but we can work together."

Vivian's mouth compressed into a tight line and she opened the door for her. "The car will take you back to your apartment," she said stiffly.

"When can I see my son again?" she asked, not leaving until she got a date.

"When it is convenient for Belleni," Vivian answered, dismissing her.

"Please, Vivian. This open-ended scheduling is cruel. Can't you imagine how hard this is? To walk away each time from my son? He's all I have to live for at this point."

At that Vivian paused and regarded Skye with an expression she'd never seen before. A sliver of compassion perhaps? Skye couldn't be sure.

"Such a flair for the dramatic," Vivian murmured but the usual rancor coating her tone was notably absent. Seeming as if going against her better judgment she said, "Tomorrow. The car will drop him off at your apartment at 8:00 a.m. You must return him by five. Not a minute later or else I will show no mercy."

Skye shuddered but accepted the offer. "Thank you, Vivian."

Her face crinkled in raw disgust. "Oh, get out. Your groveling sickens me worse than your insolence."

Skye didn't hesitate, fearing that this odd show of kindness would dissipate like mist in a strong burst of sunshine.

CHAPTER NINE

CHRISTIAN'S GRIN BROADENED as Skye came into view, clutching Nico's hand in hers. The playroom had been converted to a makeshift studio for her instruction and the kids were shifting about nervously. The girls ranged in age from seven to sixteen and the older girls wore expressions of boredom and rebellion while the younger ones were openly curious.

She went straight to Christian and as she helped Nico take off his backpack, she admitted in a tremulous voice, "I've never done anything like this. Are you sure I'm the right person for the job?"

"You're trained, and I took a chance that you don't have a record given your select clientele, though…" He paused with genuine concern, as if he hadn't actually thought this part through all the way until that moment. She smiled and assured him she didn't have a criminal record, and he continued with a relieved grin. "Oh, thank God. That would've been hard to explain. Anyway, you aren't costing the state a dime, so yeah, you're perfect. Don't worry so much. You'll be great." He looked down at Nico. "Tell your mom she's gonna be great so she'll stop freaking out."

Nico grinned up at her and gave her a thumbs-up.

"You're gonna be great, Mama," he said, and a sweet smile lit up her face.

"If you say so," she said, ruffling his hair. "Okay, you sit here with your coloring books and toys and I'll see just how cut out I am to be an instructor." She gave Christian a mock stern look as she warned over her shoulder, "If I crash and burn, this is all your fault."

"I take full responsibility because I'm not worried," he retorted, jerking his gaze sharply away from the view of her sculpted backside and pert behind. The long, clean lines of her body spoke of her background and the grace with which she carried herself further gave her away. Her hair was tucked into a bun but a few tendrils escaped, framing her bare, makeup-free face nicely, and he wondered if he'd ever seen a more beautiful woman in all his life.

He listened as she introduced herself, garnering a few interested looks when she shared her background with the New York City Ballet and when she lifted and executed a perfect pirouette with the grace of an angel lighting on earth, the few reluctant stragglers grudgingly came to attention.

"How many of you have ever thought about becoming a dancer?" A few shy hands went up. She nodded with a smile. "Well, even if you're not planning to become a professional dancer, dance is good for posture, coordination and staying in shape. I'm going to teach you some basics today. How does that sound?"

The girls nodded and clapped their hands, totally won over, just as Christian knew they would be. He leaned over to whisper to Nico, "Do you enjoy watching your mom dance?" he asked.

Nico nodded. "Sometimes she dances in the living room and it's funny. I like when she does that spinning thing. 'Cept one time she was doing that and bonked her toe on one of my toys," he confided with a giggle. "I wasn't supposed to leave it out. I got in trouble."

"One can never underestimate the importance of putting away one's toys," Christian agreed solemnly. "Especially if one's mom has a tendency to dance in the living room without warning."

Nico let another small giggle escape before saying, "I like you. You're a lot nicer than that other guy who lives with the scary lady in the big house."

Huh? "Other guy? Who might that be? A friend of your mommy's?"

"I dunno. But I live with him now. I don't like it. I like my room at Mama's better."

"You don't live with your mom?" he asked, confused.

Nico shook his head, tucking his lip under his teeth. "No. Mama said I used to live with her but then I had to move when I was little. But I get to visit her. It's fun when I visit because we go places like the park and stuff."

"What's with the scary lady? Is that the man's wife?" he asked, trying to unravel the mystery.

"I don't think so but she's always around. She pinches me and squeezes my arm real hard when I make her mad. She gives me looks like this—" Nico illustrated by narrowing his little stare in the meanest way possible for a four-year-old, which Christian found quite impressive. "And calls me a 'little bastard.'"

Christian's temper flared. Adults who called kids names and hurt them were lower than scum in his book. What did this little kid ever do to this woman to deserve that kind of treatment and why the hell did Skye let this woman around her son if she was so mean to him? Of course, Nico didn't have the answers so Christian kept his questions to himself for the time being. Instead he agreed with Nico with mock seriousness, saying, "That is pretty scary. She better be careful or her face will freeze that way."

"Really?" Hope lit up Nico's expression causing Christian to chuckle. "If that happened I'd laugh a lot. She deserves it. She makes my mama sad."

"How does she make her sad?" he asked.

Nico shrugged. "She calls Mama bad names."

"Bad names? Like what?"

Nico bit his lip, plainly caught between wanting to tell but not sure if he should. Christian didn't want to put the kid in a bad spot so he said, "Don't worry about it. She's not here right now so we don't have to talk about her anymore. Okay?"

Nico looked relieved. "Okay," he agreed with a grin. "So, do you have little kids, too?"

"Nope," Christian answered. "Maybe someday, though." Funny, he'd never really thought about it, having kids and settling down. Probably because he'd been so single-mindedly focused on getting his club off the ground, the thought of a wife and kids wasn't even a blip on his radar. And because of that, he was ultracareful in the love department. He didn't want any accidental babies popping up on his doorstep. "You close to your dad?" he asked.

Nico shook his head but he didn't look sad about it as he answered, "I don't have a dad."

Hmm…no dad. Everyone had a father. Another interesting piece of the puzzle. So if the man Nico was referring to earlier wasn't his father, who was he? For that matter, who was the scary woman?

Christian mulled the information over in his head. His gaze skipped to Skye who was showing the girls some simple stretches and when she flashed him a quick smile filled with joy and elation, he stuffed down the troubling question for later and simply returned the smile. It could wait.

SKYE'S MUSCLES WERE PROTESTING the unexpected workout but it felt like heaven. She glanced at Christian from beneath her lashes and a well of sweetness threatened to spill over into her voice as she thanked him, yet again, for the unexpected gift.

He graced her with another of those dimpled grins that caused her insides to do an uncomfortable flip and she wondered what he'd do if she simply leaned over and captured his lips with her own. What kind of kisser was he? Was he passive, allowing his partner to take control, content to let the woman dictate the pace and tone? Or did a fierce hunger to dominate lie in wait for the right moment to pounce? She suppressed a shiver that came out of nowhere and she had to wonder at herself. She couldn't remember the last time she had the luxury of discovery. She wondered if she even recalled her preference. All she knew for sure was she didn't want Belleni. It felt good to be in control of her own feelings, to allow something to unfurl naturally rather than forcing it to get the job done.

"Everything okay?" Christian asked when he saw her frown.

"Yeah," she assured him with a bright smile to chase away the shadows that might be lurking in her gaze. "So I cleared my schedule for today…what do you say we put together a picnic and claim a spot in the park?"

He checked his watch. "Sure. I got some time. There's a little market not far from here we could pick up a few things. We don't even need to take a cab. We can walk."

"Perfect." She clasped Nico's hand and they set off at a leisurely pace. After a few minutes, she said, "You know it was so great to work with the kids. I never considered teaching dance before but I think I might actually be good at it." She risked a look his way, curious if he agreed.

"You looked like a natural to me," he said. "Tell me why you don't dance professionally any longer?"

She knew this question was bound to pop up sooner or later but she'd hoped that maybe more time would pass before it did. It was difficult to talk about her time before Belleni came into her life, when dancing was everything. But she felt she owed Christian something for the gift he'd given her. She drew a deep breath before beginning.

"As I told you previously, I came to New York to dance with the New York City Ballet. At first I was doing very well. I managed to catch the eye of the choreographer and in spite of the fact that some of the other girls had better dance credits under their belt, I was starting to land bigger roles. Then I was cast as one of the Auroras in *Sleeping Beauty* and I thought for sure I'd died and gone to heaven. It was a major deal. Then, one day in rehearsal when I went to do a grand jeté somehow I landed wrong and tore my ACL. The surgeon said it was the worst tear he'd ever seen and even though I had surgery to repair it and followed up with physical therapy, it remained weak. The verdict was clear—my professional dancing career was over."

She finished with a halting breath, the loss of her career still a sore spot with her even though it'd been five years since that awful day. She could tell he was doing the math, speculating on what happened next in her life. She'd have to explain Nico somehow but she wasn't quite ready so she quickly put the spotlight on him. "So, you're a bartender at Martini...how'd you end up there?" she asked.

He caught her not-so-subtle deflection but decided to follow her lead for which she was grateful. He smiled. "Would you believe I came to New York to be a bartender?"

She didn't want to offend him but her hesitation gave her away. It was hard for her to imagine wanting to become a bartender. To her it seemed a job you fell into due to circumstance rather than seeking it out. Sort of like what happened to her with her current profession. "Why?" she asked tentatively, cringing at the bald question. "I'm sorry. I didn't mean it like that..."

"No, it's okay," he assured her, sealing her belief that he was quite possibly not only the most good-looking but nicest guy she'd met in a long time. "I wanted to become a bartender because I wanted to know everything about how a club works and the bartender is a good place to start. I plan to own my own club someday soon and because of my bartending experience I know what it's like behind the bar. I know what to look for if an employee is dipping into the till and I know what to avoid in personality types for management. It's been an educational experience that was exactly what I was looking for. With that said, I'm ready to make the transition from employee to boss."

She arched her brow. "Really? That's pretty ambitious in this town. I mean, you have to know that start-up businesses, particularly restaurants or bars, have a fifty-fifty shot of failing in the first year." Oh, God, what a downer. She nearly clapped her hand over her mouth in dismay. "I'm sorry. That was so rude of me. I just meant to say…well, actually there's no other way to say it. But I hope you know I mean it in the nicest way possible."

"Trust me, I know the statistics. My business partner and I are well aware of the risks. That's why we've set away two years' worth of payroll in the bank."

"Two years?" she murmured. "That's a lot of money."

"Yeah, it is. But with two years' payroll we won't have to stress about the bottom line so much as building a solid reputation. The money will come in time. I have faith."

Faith…she knew all about that word. She also knew that after faith failed, came misery and disillusion but she wisely kept that to herself. No sense in raining on his parade when they barely knew one another. She kind of liked the idea of seeing him again, crazy as it seemed, and she didn't want to run him off with her cynicism. "I hope it works out for you," she said, truly meaning it. "Following a dream is a ride worth taking."

Amiable silence stretched between them and Skye basked in the happy moment to insulate her against the bad times that were surely on the horizon.

After the market they made the trek to the sun-dappled park and after convincing Nico to eat a few bites, the boy dashed off to the play structure that was within her vision, leaving her alone with Christian.

Suddenly her nerves jumped and she almost hopped to her feet to follow her son. It seemed safer over there than sitting so close to Christian, eating out-of-season, exorbitantly priced grapes.

"Why doesn't Nico live with you?" he asked, startling her with his frank question.

She stalled and her brain blanked when she searched for a plausible reason. As the silence stretching between them became awkward, he must've realized an answer wasn't forthcoming and he looked away. "You must have your reasons," he said. "But I gotta tell you it doesn't sound like Nico is in a great environment. Whoever the mean, scary lady is…she's abusive to him."

Skye choked down the rising lump in her throat but held her composure by the thinnest thread. He had no idea how it ripped her heart from her chest to know she couldn't keep her baby safe—that every night her son wet the bed because he was terrified of his surroundings. "Do you always butt your nose into other people's business or is this something you save for me?" she asked coolly, masking her pain with ice.

"Good question," he said, as if to himself. The furrow in his brow told her he was just as perplexed as she was prickly about the situation. He shook his head. "You're right it's none of my business how you choose to raise your son. I just thought…I don't know, that maybe you cared."

"I do care," she said, heat rising in her cheeks. Hating the idea that he thought she might be flippant about her son's welfare, she admitted in a tight voice, "But maybe my hands are tied," before she could stop herself.

"What do you mean?" he asked, those intense blue eyes burning into hers, searching for the source of her outburst.

She collected herself quickly, forcing a smile but it felt brittle and she doubted it came off as sincere. "How did we get here? We were having a nice afternoon. Let's go back to that," she suggested.

"Excellent advice even if it's improbable," he muttered, the threat of a dark scowl hovering in his expression. "You have a choice, Skye. If not for yourself, for your son."

Skye wiped the sticky grape juice from her fingers, her temper rising at his judgment but she wasn't about to make a scene here in the park. Aside from the fact that Nico might hear her, she had to be careful not to draw attention to herself. Belleni had eyes everywhere. She would never presume that she was safe from his prying influence anywhere in the city. "You have no right to judge me," she said quietly, though she fairly vibrated with anger and hurt. "I appreciate the opportunity to work with the children but I think we should end our acquaintance."

She rose from the grass, intending to walk away

and collect her son but Christian jumped up and caught her hand, the contact sizzling up her arm. She gasped. "What are you doing?" she demanded in a harsh whisper.

"I don't know," Christian admitted, and looking as if he didn't much like it, either. "I'm sorry. Don't stop working with the kids because I can't keep my feelings to myself."

Skye edged her tongue along her bottom lip, catching the residual sweetness from the grapes and his gaze followed the movement. His stare widened ever so slightly as if he were trying to hide his reaction but Skye was sensitive to body language and she picked it up quite readily. Of course, she wasn't accustomed to her own body reacting in kind. She looked away, if only to catch her breath without being too obvious. She shrugged. "I guess I could continue for a while," she said, looking back at him, gauging his expression. Aside from the delicious rush of pheromones there was also the tension from walking a dangerous line. What if Belleni caught them here at the park? He was notoriously territorial when it suited him and lately it seemed to suit him a lot when it came to Skye. Discomfited with the thought of being spied upon, she put some distance between herself and Christian. "But if I do, we need to keep our distance. I'm not looking for a boyfriend of any kind."

"And I'm not looking for a girlfriend," he countered. "So we're on the same page."

"Right. Good." At least it ought to be. So why

did his declaration send a sharp pain right into her chest bone? Maybe because it would've been nice to be able to pretend she was a normal girl even when he knew she wasn't. "Glad we're both clear in our expectations."

They broke eye contact, each retreating into the privacy of their thoughts and Skye secretly lamented the change between them. For a moment she'd almost remembered what it felt like to be a woman free to flirt with the possibility of something bigger than herself, something that made her heart sing like her feet used to dance.

The loss of it was what hurt the most.

CHAPTER TEN

CHRISTIAN WAS STILL playing that last moment with Skye through his head as he entered the upscale restaurant, already ten minutes late for his dinner date, but he couldn't quite wipe away the disturbing realization that he was fighting an ever-growing attraction to her.

When he closed his eyes he saw her face, smiling with joy at her son. When he saw her favor her left side, he burned with the need to find the guy who had assaulted her and rearrange his fat face. But he didn't want any of those things. He started off wanting to help her, pure and simple. Somehow his motivation had morphed into something deeper without his consent and he didn't know what to do about it.

All he knew was he ought to pull back fast. He wasn't Richard Gere and she wasn't Julia Roberts and this sure as hell wasn't their version of *Pretty Woman.*

She hadn't once plainly stated to him that she wanted out of the business and that single thing made him stiffen and want to take a huge step away from her. Yet, at this very moment, when he should be considering the possibilities of this evening, he was thinking of her.

Good going, Holt. Way to introduce a major wrench in the machine. He sighed and headed in the direction of his friend.

Gage caught his eye and there was definitely irritation reflecting back at him but he didn't call him on his tardiness, just turned and introduced him to his date for the night as well as his own.

"Irena, Madeline, this is my friend and business partner, Christian Holt."

Christian shook hands with both ladies, surmising that the leggy brunette Madeline was Gage's date and the less leggy and rounder brunette was Christian's date for the evening. "So nice to meet you both," he said politely.

His date stepped forward and linked her arm through his, clearly pleased with what she saw and Christian chuckled at her bold action. She had chutzpah that's for sure, he noted.

"You're adorable," Irena declared, stopping a moment to squeeze his bicep, her voice appreciative. "And so fit! I think men should be hard and women should be soft. So we're nearly perfect together."

He laughed and caught Gage's eye. "Can't argue with that now, can I? Shall we go to our table or hit the bar first?"

"Whatever the ladies would like," he said, his gaze devouring Madeline's figure, not that Gage could be blamed. She sizzled in that red, form-fitting dress;

hell, even Irena was eye-catching in her black dress. His date was curvy in all the right places and he wasn't above letting his stare rove the hills and valleys but unfortunately, Irena was battling for position when Skye had already won the competition, much to his consternation.

Still, the night was young and Irena seemed the sort who liked a good time so he wasn't about to leave early.

But even though his intentions were to have fun and forget about everything else for the moment, it was impossible to actually follow through with that plan and several times his date caught him with his focus elsewhere.

"And that was the absolute last time I shot fire out of my eyeballs," Irena finished, laughing as he startled when he actually heard what she'd said. "Just checking to see if you're paying attention. Where are you? Because you're certainly not sitting here with me."

His cheeks heated and he apologized for being rude. "I'm a bit distracted. You were saying?" he prompted, trying to make amends but she was a good sport and waved him away.

"Don't worry about it. So how do you know Gage?" she asked, sipping at her drink and shooting a glance in Gage's direction where he was chatting with his date.

"Ah, well, I met him when I came to New York. We were roommates for a time and became friends by default. Now we work together at Martini and we're trying to open our own nightclub."

"He's a nice guy," she admitted, almost reluctantly. Her smile brightened as she fastened on a new subject. "Want to tell me what's on your mind? I'm a decent listener."

He laughed. "It's nothing. Just work stuff," he lied. He didn't see the point in talking to his date about another woman and honestly, he didn't quite know his own feelings on that score, except that he was wildly drawn to Skye, so he thought it best to keep it private. But he felt it was nice of Irena to offer so he did the same. "Tell me about you," he suggested amiably, which she did with enthusiasm.

The night wore on and it was all Christian could do to seem engaged and interested when in fact, he'd begun to wish he'd begged off. Irena chattered nonstop and when she wasn't going on about something in her life, she was touching him. At first it was playful, but then as the drinks kept coming, she became more sexual in her advances, which was a shame because he'd felt a real friendly connection with her at the beginning of the evening.

It wasn't that he didn't care for aggressive women, in fact, he liked a woman who knew how to take control but Skye was in his head and therefore there was nothing going on in his pants and Irena's attempt at changing his mind was becoming downright irritating. He caught Gage's eyes and motioned for him to follow him to the bar.

"What do you think of Irena?" Gage asked, clearly buzzed from the shots of Jameson whiskey he'd had earlier. "She's pretty hot, huh? I told you I wouldn't steer you wrong. And if I'm not mistaken, she likes you. You might even get laid tonight if you play your cards right," he said, nudging him with an elbow. "I'll bet Irena is wild in the sack."

"Are you sure you're with the right date?"

"What do you mean?" he asked, nonplussed.

"All you're doing is talking about how hot my date is when your own date is pretty good-looking, too. I just wondered..."

Gage laughed at the idea but Christian sensed a little bit of nervousness underneath the self-assured sound. "Irena is a nice girl and she's not hard on the eyes but she's nothing compared to Madeline. I mean, did you see those legs? They go straight up to her neck. Niiice."

"True. But Irena...she's got those big, plump breasts that make you want to bury your face in them. And that booty? Damn." He was totally playing Gage. He had no more interest in Irena than Gage truly had in Madeline but it was entertaining watching Gage pretend that he was hot for the leggy one when in fact, he was eyeing her friend. He wondered if Irena knew. Hell, chances were neither of them knew how the other felt. People were surprisingly thick when it came to their own love radar. He signaled for the bartender to close his tab. "So how'd you meet Irena and Madeline?" he asked.

"I met them both at the gym. They were playing racquetball and I was waiting for the court. Well, I should say Irena was playing while Madeline was running into the walls a lot. It's those long legs. She's like a giraffe in an enclosed space." He chuckled ruefully but his eyes lit up when he added about Irena, "Now that girl is like a badger. She's vicious out there on the court. I played her once and she kicked my ass."

Yep. Definitely had the hots for Irena. So why the subterfuge? He was mildly curious to find the answer but he was more interested in getting home so he could call Skye. Gage would have to figure out his own love life. He collected his credit card and Gage frowned in dismay. "What the hell? You're leaving? The night's just getting started," he protested.

"Maybe for you, buddy. I have an early morning commitment. Tell Irena I had a great time but I have to run."

"You tell her. You can't just skip out on her. That's rude," he said.

"Here's the deal, if I go back to our table and tell her I want to leave she's going to try and convince me to stay and I don't want to hurt her feelings. Besides… I'm not sure I'm the one she wants," he said, letting that sink in for a moment.

Gage frowned. "You think she's a lesbian?" he asked a bit distressed, which made Christian laugh.

He clapped Gage on the shoulder. "She's definitely not a lesbian. I think she likes you, buddy."

"Me?" His voice strained a little but his eyes warmed too much to be faking it. "Really? Are you sure?"

"I'm only sure of death and taxes but even when her hands were on me—" Gage scowled and Christian knew his instincts weren't off base, the guy was totally into Irena "—she was looking over at you to catch your reaction."

And if teenage jealousy tricks didn't say "I have the hots for you," Christian wasn't sure what did. Amazing how it didn't matter how long it'd been since you were in the school yard, old habits died hard. Well, at least he'd outgrown the "hey, I like you so I'm going to pull your ponytail" courtship style. "Good luck, my friend," he said, pocketing his credit card. "Make me look good…or bad. Whatever works for you."

"Christian, wait—"

"Nope. It's all you, buddy. Don't blow it. You never know, she could be the mother of your future children."

He caught the reflexive movement of Gage swallowing and he grinned. *Better you than me, my friend.*

Actually, he envied his friend. At least with his date what you saw was what he got, unlike Skye. Why couldn't it have been simple with her? If the circumstances were different and she'd remained a dancer, he'd have been tripping over himself to get a date with her. She had the looks of a supermodel and a body to match. Superficially, she definitely had the goods that would make his head turn. And if that wasn't enough, the love for her son elevated her in his opinion even more.

Except that wasn't the reality between them. The fact was, as easygoing as he liked to consider himself, and a man who subscribed to the motto To each his own, he could not reconcile the fact that Skye sold herself for money. Sure, it looked different on the outside than what his mother did but strip away the luxury and the expensive trappings and it was the same dirty trade.

And he hated it.

Which only served to confuse him about his feelings for Skye. The worst part was he couldn't seem to walk away—even though he knew he should.

VIVIAN LOCKED HER BEDROOM door and crossed to her walk-in closet where she went straight to a box and pulled it down.

The box, a plain shoe box, was incongruous with the designer labels hanging from fine wooden hangers but hidden inside were Vivian's treasures.

Today was an awful day, she reflected calmly, going to her vanity and placing the box on the surface so she could crack the lid and sift through the contents. She cursed the day Skye D'Lane entered her life. She should've recognized her for the cancer she was but like all malignancies, the danger started out small and insignificant.

Belleni had sought out the fallen ballerina after coming across a small newspaper clipping about her injury and subsequent replacement as one of the New York City Ballet Auroras. There were three doing the show on a rotating basis and Skye had landed the coveted part after only dancing with the company for a year. Belleni had been mesmerized, saying, "I shall add an angel to our ranks."

Ugh. His angel. And her nightmare.

She suppressed a sigh of irritation and pulled a hospital bracelet from the box. She traced her finger along the worn plastic, the only memento she'd ever been able to keep of the child that was never meant to be.

What kind of mother would she have been? She liked to think she would've been firm yet loving; doting yet with boundaries. She dropped the wristband. Too bad she'd never know.

Of course, aside from the initial shock of it all, she'd never really dwelled on the past, until that little parasite came into their lives. Then everything had changed.

She'd long believed that she alone held a special place in Belleni's heart. How could she not? She knew him better than anyone. She managed all aspects of his business and together they had amassed a considerable fortune through discipline and hard work. Managing the kind of secrecy the business required was no small feat. And everything was working fabulously until she came along.

The first time she'd seen that light flare in his eyes twisted her heart and curdled her stomach but she'd told herself it was a momentary infatuation, easily dismissed.

But then the child came. Vivian had waited to hear the words he'd said to her delivered to that whore but they never came. In fact, he seemed delighted with the idea of Skye carrying his child. That alone was a knife to her back but now, he was talking about acknowledging the boy as his son. "Ridiculous," she muttered to herself. He was giving Skye the power to bring him and by proxy, her, down. Why? What was so special about Skye? Why did everyone fall under her spell? A vision of Skye appeared in her mind with her lithe yet supple figure and she couldn't help twisting in self-loathing. Skye had the effortless benefit of youth while Vivian waged a constant battle with the clock. Her breasts were no longer plump and full; her skin no longer shone with vitality.

A sudden, lone tear pricked her eye and she wiped it away, her thoughts narrowing to a razor point. Here she was marinating in self-pity in her room when she could be doing something proactive to improve her situation.

The key to returning things to how they should be was to get rid of Skye. Five years of misery was enough for anyone to suffer and Vivian had suffered the most.

The woman must go. And frankly, she thought,

stuffing the lid on the box tightly, she didn't care if she left alive…or dead.

And that went for the boy, too.

CHAPTER ELEVEN

CHRISTIAN FOUGHT THE URGE to adjust his tie, knowing it was plain nerves that prompted the itch instead of a true wardrobe malfunction. He took care to dress in his finest suit and shoes, even brushed and styled his hair for this meeting and because there was so much riding on it, he was about ready to jump out of his skin.

The man he was about to meet at the upscale coffee house was Frank Rocco, a contact of Gage's that, according to Gage, had plenty of money, liked to invest in start-up companies with promise and was looking for a new project. If Christian and Gage managed to slide into that coveted spot, they'd have their club up and running within three months. That tasty carrot dangling in front of him kept him from reconsidering bringing in a third party. It wasn't ideal to have another partner—silent or otherwise—but he wasn't in a position to turn away a good prospect.

His cell phone came to life in his pocket and he took a quick look. He groaned when he saw the caller ID—Mama Jo—and he didn't have time to explain why he'd canceled his scheduled visit. No doubt she wanted to reschedule and he couldn't give her a solid answer just yet. Regretfully, he sent her to voice mail and ignored the wash of guilt that followed. He would call her back right after the meeting, he made himself promise. He truly missed Mama Jo, but as she would say, he had a funny way of showing it. He hadn't been home in a while. Life kept throwing him curve balls and he had to be around to knock them back. She understood. Most of the time. But this last cancellation, he'd heard more than disappointment in her tone. Can't think about that now. Gotta focus on the here and now and that included the man who held the key to all his dreams.

Who just happened to be sitting at the table farthest from the door, in a little pocket near the window, sipping his espresso with a contemplative expression. Frank Rocco was as Gage described, distinguished, well-dressed, yet seemingly down-to-earth and Christian's nervousness dissipated.

He smiled as he extended his hand. "Mr. Rocco? Christian Holt. Nice to meet you, sir."

"A pleasure," Frank Rocco said in his softly accented voice, clasping his hand in a firm shake as Christian sat opposite him. He gestured to the barista and she brought something hot, dark and rich to his table. "Best kept secret in New York," he shared as Christian sipped at his drink. "Eh?"

Christian choked down the strong brew, not particularly fond of coffee in general, but put a brave face on, not wanting to offend his potential business partner right off the bat. "Smooth," he said. And likely to put hair on his chest if it wasn't lightly covered already. "Thank you for agreeing to listen to my proposal. I know your time is valuable so I'll get right to the point." Frank inclined his head ever so slightly as if to say he appreciated his candid style and Christian took that as a good sign as he continued, "Gage and I have the operating expenses covered, we even have the business location scouted, distributors in line and a solid business plan…what we don't have is someone to provide the venture capital. We aren't looking for someone who will babysit the operation but rather someone who believes in our plan and is willing to see it through with us. Gage believes you might be the one we're looking for."

A shrewd light entered the older man's gaze as he accepted the detailed business plan from Christian. "Why me?" he asked as he flipped through the pages. "There must be a handful of investors milling around the city, looking for a good project. What drew you to me?"

"Easy. You have a reputation for being solid, honest and the best part in my book, profitable. We're looking to make a profit, therefore we're looking for someone who has a track record with making it work in a tough environment. Clubs come and go. But the ones with staying power make mad money. We think we have what it takes to make it."

"Confident," Frank mused. "But every green businessman with stars in his eyes thinks he's the one who's going to be the success instead of the statistic. Tell me why you're different."

Christian leaned forward, the intensity he felt in his gut shining in his stare as he said, "Because I know it takes more than hard work, more than desire, more than strong business sense to make it a success…it takes *obsession.* I will eat, drink, breathe nothing but what it takes to make it work."

"Obsession," Frank said, clearly amused but there was something else in his tone, something that smacked of respect. He narrowed his gaze at Christian. "What of a personal life? A special lady friend? A wife, perhaps?"

Christian hesitated, his thoughts flying inexplicably to Skye, which he shook off with effort. Now was not the time to show any cracks in his resolve. He didn't know why he thought of Skye. They barely knew one another and he knew for a certainty, she wasn't the woman he'd feel comfortable having a relationship with…yet, there was something there. Maybe it was simple hormones and whatever it was would fade. He couldn't bank on something that wasn't actually real at the moment when the man holding the key to his hopes and dreams was sitting in front of him, watching him, waiting for an answer to his seemingly simple query. He grinned. "Mr. Rocco… I'm finally standing on the precipice of what could be the culmination of hopes and dreams…I'm not going to throw it all away over a woman."

"Truer words were never spoken," Frank agreed,

though there was a split second of regret reflected in his eyes that was gone so fast Christian was sure he imagined it. Drawing away, he rapped his knuckles lightly against the business plan and said, "This is good stuff. I like your style. I will be in touch."

Christian nodded, elation zinging through his brain at the positive vibes he was getting from the older man. He was nearly close enough to his dreams to reach out and touch them. He'd imagined this moment for so long it almost seemed unreal. "I look forward to your call," he said, rising.

Frank chuckled and after adjusting his cuffs, let himself out to the awaiting Bentley idling at the curb.

Christian watched as the car melted into the busy traffic and couldn't stop the grin. Good things were about to happen. He could feel it.

SKYE WALKED INTO THE MAKESHIFT dance studio and faced the fifteen young faces staring back at her. Their first class had gone well enough considering none of the children had ever had any formal dance training. There were a handful who actually showed promise. It was delightful to see their eyes light up and their bodies respond with instinct to the dance steps as if they were born to do it. She remembered her first dance class and how her heart had sang as she learned the steps. She felt privileged to introduce these girls to such a classic art form. And to that end, she'd brought some supplies.

"Gather around, girls," she instructed, dropping the large bag to the floor. "I've brought you something."

The girls crowded around her, eyeing the bag with open curiosity. Skye smiled as she unzipped it. "Dancers need proper dance supplies. I found some old leotards and ballet slippers in my closet and then went to a few dance studios throughout the city and gathered some donated leotards. I tried to guesstimate your sizes by memory," she said, smiling as the girls rummaged through the bag, exclaiming as they found a size that would work for them. After everyone had something in their hands, she dismissed them to change. A sweetness born of satisfaction formed her smile and she thought of Christian. His kindness warmed her heart in a way that she didn't have time to dwell upon.

The girls returned and she clapped her hands with pleasure. "You look like dancers!" she exclaimed, eliciting shy smiles. "Now we can begin."

She took the girls through an hour of instruction and after they were all worn out, but still smiling, she ended the class with a promise to see them next week.

Skye was packing her bag when a girl named Payton came up to her. "Are you going to stay our teacher or are you going to bail on us eventually?"

Skye quieted at the pointed question. "I…well, I don't know how long I'll be here. It just depends on how long I'm invited to stay, I imagine," she answered honestly. She didn't want to give the girl a false promise. After all those children had been through she wasn't about to betray them further by lying. She held her breath until the girl seemed to accept the answer.

"I knew you wouldn't stick around forever...but thanks for being honest."

Payton turned to leave and Skye stopped her with a gentle hand on her shoulder. "You know, I'd really love to see you continue to dance. You've got something and it's called talent. Not everyone can dance like you can." Payton stared, unsure of what to do with that kind of praise. Skye smiled. "Just keep coming to class at the very least. Okay?"

Payton bit her bottom lip but finally allowed a short smile as she nodded and said, "Okay. See you next week. Oh, and thanks for the leotard and ballet slippers. They feel good. Like we're real dancers or something," she added sheepishly, then bolted as if she'd said too much and risked further embarrassment. Skye didn't try to stop her, just grinned and finished packing her bag.

"You're a natural," Christian said, startling her. She smiled in welcome, happier than she should be to see him. She met him at the door where he lounged against the door frame. "You got plans after this?"

"Not for a bit, why?" she answered, ignoring the private thrill that danced tiny fingers along her skin in anticipation.

"I want to show you something," he said, a hint of playfulness in his grin.

She slung her dance bag over her shoulder. "Such as?"

"Just say yes and I'll show you."

Skye vacillated between desperately wanting to go with him and needing to keep her distance. Belleni expected her back to her apartment by 5:00 p.m. or else he'd send Vincent to track her down and if that happened, there would be consequences. Once she'd been late because the subway train had broken down but Belleni wouldn't listen. He punished her as he always did, by withholding her son from her. It was the most foolproof way of keeping her towed and tethered without having to lock her into the apartment. She nipped her bottom lip, unsure of what to do until Christian lifted her dance bag from her shoulders and she had to stop the flutters that followed the chivalrous gesture. She couldn't remember the last time someone took a true interest in her comfort or feelings.

"If you're up for a shared taxi ride, I think you'll like what I have to show you," he said.

"What is it?" she asked.

"Don't like surprises?"

"Not especially," she answered truthfully. In her experience surprises tended to leave her with bruises at the worst and an unfortunate evening at the most benign. Besides, she'd never been one for mysteries. "I don't know you well enough to agree to go somewhere without prior knowledge of the destination. That's just reckless and I have Nico to think of."

Sobering quickly, he said, "Skye, I would never hurt you."

She knew that and it wasn't because he'd already saved her life. It was because of what she saw in his heart that she knew if it were in his power, he'd always do what he could to ensure her safety. The knowledge was at once sweet and brutal. A lump rose in her throat at the cruelty of her situation and it gave her one more reason to hate Belleni. Not that she needed another. She already had a boatload of reasons.

Christian must've sensed her waffling for he said, "All right. How about this…a compromise. I will tell you where we're going, if not why we're going there. How's that?"

She considered his offer. He waited for her answer, watching her with those killer blues from beneath long, dusky eyelashes that would make any woman jealous for their length and she relented with a shake of her head. "Okay," she agreed, eliciting a wide grin from Christian. "But I only have two hours to spare. I have to get Nico before five. Promise we'll be back in time?" Nico was with Belleni but she needed a plausible excuse because she couldn't imagine actually telling Christian the truth about her curfew.

"I promise." He stepped aside, holding the door for her and her heart tripped a beat. She flashed him a tiny, appreciative smile and followed him to the street. It occurred to her as they hailed a cab, she couldn't remember the last time she felt so free, so normal. And she drank it up like a woman dying from thirst.

CHRISTIAN DIDN'T KNOW why he wanted to share this with Skye but the desire to fold her into his arms was equally strong. He could name the reason for the latter—she was probably the sexiest woman he'd ever met and the thought of touching her in something more than friendship made his teeth ache, along with other parts of his anatomy—but the driving force behind his invitation was something far more elusive and seductive.

They pulled up to an abandoned warehouse a few blocks from Central Park, on West Fifty-second Street. It was a busy street with plenty of upscale action in the form of restaurants, stores and even a post office outlet and Christian grinned as they exited the cab. He took a chance and clasped her hand to pull her toward the building. Her astonished expression gave way to puzzlement as he went straight to the front double doors. "What are you doing? Do you own this building?" she asked, glancing around as if afraid of being arrested.

"I don't actually own the building…yet…but Gage is a commercial real estate broker when he's not bartending and this just happens to be one of his properties," he explained, giving the lock a jiggle when the key stuck. It clicked open and he gave the door a firm push. It opened with a creak that was surely heard for miles and they slipped inside.

Dust motes danced in the stale, cold air and it smelled of old timber, age and industrial storage. Weak, watery light shone through windows fogged with years of grime and a fine layer of dirt settled on every surface. He led her into the back where the remnants of a bygone era lay rusting, disintegrating or the opposite, remaining stalwart, but useless, against the passage of time.

"What was this place?" she asked, her brow furrowing slightly, rubbing at her nose from the dust. "And why are we here?"

Christian opened his arms wide and spun in a slow circle. "This," he said, "is the place where I want to open my very own nightclub. I met with a venture capitalist today and I think he really believed in our vision for the club. If he decides to invest, we could be up and running within three months."

"Three months? Are you sure? It's pretty old… and dirty."

He laughed. "Ye of little faith. Nothing a bit of elbow grease couldn't fix. We've already had a building inspector come out and give us a report on the structural integrity—we'd need to bring the piping up to code and whatnot but the bones of this place are solid. This building has been a lot of things in its lifetime."

Her gaze traveled the open beams and steel framing. "Such as?"

He hesitated before answering but decided to go with the truth. "Well, for example, at one time this place was a brothel in the late 1800s." When she flashed him a look but continued her silent perusal, he added quickly, "Well, in its next incarnation it was a pressroom for a newspaper and then in its most recent life, it was used for industrial storage, which would account for the odd oil splashes here and there in the dirt. It might've even been a garage in the '30s, I'm not sure, I'd have to check. But a place like this has a rich history and I knew the minute I saw it that it was going to be the location of my club." He gestured, lifting the tarp covering something long and bulky. "And this right here was how I knew for sure," he said, revealing a very old, ornate, soft maple bartop with dark, rich tones and an aged finish. Skye sucked in a surprised breath and came to get a better look. "Gorgeous, isn't it?" When she nodded, he said, "When Gage and I researched the building we found archival photos of this bar in the saloon that originally inhabited the building. And somehow, through all the years, it survived. I'm guessing that the owners either never knew about it or thought to sell it eventually and just never did. Gage and I found it in the basement with a bunch of other stuff."

"It's amazing," she said, running her fingers lightly down the ornate carving. "Handcrafted. Wow, it's beautiful."

"Yeah, that's what we thought, too. We want to restore it and put it into the club."

Her eyes shone as her mouth formed a wondrous smile. "I think that's a great idea. It would give the club automatic history and that could be a selling point. New Yorkers love something with character." She glanced around with a speculative expression as she asked, "So what else do you plan to do with the place?"

His insides warmed at her interest. "Well, the first two stories will be the nightclub and the top floor will be administrative offices. We hired an architect to draft some plans and a designer to create a vision. We want to incorporate the building's history along with a fresh new look, so modern yet classic, edgy without being trendy."

"Nice. So your clientele…?"

"Kind of like Martini, upscale, with established incomes who enjoy a bit of refinement with their entertainment."

She nodded, an odd expression flitting across her face but it cleared and she offered him a smile that spoke of her opinion. "It's a great idea. I have a picture in my head and it's gorgeous. I think you might really have something here."

"Thanks," he said, her approval important to him for reasons he didn't want to examine too closely. "I've lived and breathed this dream for so long I can't remember what it was like to be without the vision in my head."

"That's how I felt about dance," she said wistfully. "It takes a certain amount of obsession to make dreams come true."

He grinned. "That's exactly how I feel. I definitely have the obsession part. My friend Gage said if he didn't see dollar signs in my eyes whenever we talked about the club he would've found a different friend. According to him, there's more to life than business."

She risked a short smile. "Not for some."

He agreed. "Not for those who cannot accept failure."

"When I danced the world disappeared. I didn't mind the broken toes, the bunions, the strict diet… because when I took the stage I became the part and it felt like magic."

"What was it like to dance as Aurora?"

Her eyes shone with remembered joy that was only slightly dimmed by sadness as she said, "Incomparable."

"I wish I could've seen you dance," he said.

Skye's mouth trembled with a smile. "Me, too."

Standing in the milky light, surrounded by the promise of his dreams, he stared at the woman before him, fighting a hunger that had him by the short hairs. He wanted to tell her how beautiful she looked, yet he couldn't—or wouldn't—form the words. How many other men had uttered those same words to her as she offered herself for their entertainment? The thought made him twist in disgust but it didn't cool the heat building between them. He knew she felt it, too. It didn't help that he'd already seen her naked. There were no barriers to his imagination. In his mind, the only place it was safe to touch her, his mouth tasted her bare skin; his fingers explored every inch. Most times he shut down those thoughts before they took hold. But right here, now, he couldn't seem to muster the willpower.

He stepped toward her, drawn to her without thought. She didn't stop him, but her eyes widened and the tip of her tongue darted to moisten her lips. The small motion nearly caused his knees to buckle. "I have a confession to make," he began, his voice straining as his body tightened.

"And what would that be?" she asked, her eyes wide and luminous.

Instead of answering, he simply dipped his head and brushed a soft but firm kiss against the sweetness of her mouth. It'd been his intention to only do that but once his lips touched hers the contact ignited a firestorm that he couldn't quite control. Her body melted against his, pressing in all the right places, her softness fit perfectly against his hardened planes, and as she clutched his lower back, her fingers curling against his shirt, he felt his whole world tilt.

And somewhere, far off in the functioning recesses of his brain echoed his answer to the question posed by Frank Rocco earlier that day.

I'm finally standing on the precipice of what could be the culmination of hopes and dreams…I'm not going to throw it all away over a woman.

CHAPTER TWELVE

SKYE CLUNG TO CHRISTIAN, drinking in the sensation that felt wholly unfamiliar though she'd done this particular dance a million times. Every other man's touch faded into nothing as Christian claimed her mouth in a searing yet gentle kiss that she wished would never end.

Of course, this complicated matters, she realized belatedly.

They slowly broke contact. Her chest rose rapidly with the exertion of her heart beating against her breastbone. Neither spoke, each processing what had just happened and the implications.

He grimaced, looking as if someone had just pounded a nail in his foot, and she knew how he felt.

"That was a mistake," she said quickly, her words tasting strangely hollow.

"Yeah," he agreed, frowning in distress. "I'm sorry..."

She bit her lip. Resentment raised its ugly head as she lamented the fact that she wasn't free to explore her feelings about Christian. If Belleni knew where she was he'd have Christian permanently removed from the planet and he'd be sure to punish her soundly for her betrayal. Belleni allowed men the use of her body, at his discretion, but if she were to give her heart…she suppressed a frightened shudder at the thought. She wanted Christian to have the opportunity to make his way in the world. She wanted him to open his club and have an honest shot at success. That surely wasn't possible with her around.

She took a small step away from Christian and made a show of looking at her watch. "We have to get back. It's almost time to pick up Nico. Thank you for sharing this with me. I hope it works out for you. For what it's worth I think you've got something good."

"Wait." Christian followed her, grasping her arms. "I feel I should explain myself."

"Why?"

"Because I feel bad," he admitted.

She smiled. "It was just a kiss. Don't beat yourself up about it."

But it wasn't just a kiss. Not to her, and judging by the storm gathering behind his eyes, not to him, either. On one hand she was relieved to know she wasn't alone in her feelings, but on the other hand, it only served to make her want to run far and fast for both their sakes.

"I can't have a relationship with you," he said, looking pained. "I just…can't."

She stiffened and pulled out of his grasp. "And I wasn't offering one."

"Your feelings are hurt," he stated, his mouth tightening with regret. "I'm sorry. It's just that—"

"No explanations are necessary," she retorted, turning on her heel. "I'm serious about the time. I can't be late to pick up Nico."

He followed her out the door and locked up. He still insisted on carrying her dance bag as they hailed a cab. She half expected him to pick up the argument as they drove away but he seemed to be mulling over what had happened and what had been said. She appreciated his silence but deep down, a well of sadness lurked. She ached in places that she'd thought for sure were dead. Her damn heart thudded heavily in her chest, reminding her that she had no freedom, no choice, but if she did, she would've chosen to see where things could go with Christian.

She swallowed the sad sigh. *If only...*

BELLENI HOLLERED FOR VIVIAN, his tone impatient. She quickened her step, rounding the corner with a question on her lips. "What is it?" she asked, perturbed. He'd interrupted her as she was rearranging the flowers recently delivered. The huge spray looked as if a kindergartner had arranged it rather than the high-end florist she paid an exorbitant amount to have fresh flowers delivered every day to the house. She pulled off her gardening gloves with practiced care and regarded Belleni patiently.

"I need your opinion," he stated.

Of course he did. The man was hopeless. She smiled indulgently. "What seems to be the issue?"

"I think it's time that Skye move here," he said, causing the bottom of Vivian's world to disintegrate.

She stiffened. "It sounds as if you've made your decision. What did you need my assistance for?"

His smile became calculating. "You can be quite persuasive when you are properly motivated."

"True. But I do not see myself finding the appropriate motivation to move Skye *and* Nico into this house." My home. *Our* home, she wanted to cry. "It's bad enough having that little bastard running around."

"Vivian, I am not asking your permission," he reminded her quietly and she shot him a dark, wounded look. How dare he. After all they'd shared? They were a team, better than husband and wife or mere business partners. They shared the burden of secrets that bound them together. What greater bond was there? Perhaps if she'd ignored Belleni's demand that she abort their child all those years ago, he'd have fallen in love with her instead of the broken dancer. Was it only the child? Or were Skye and the child simply a means to the end with a bonus of having an heir?

Belleni's face softened and his eyes warmed with compassion as if he'd seen into her heartache and reacted with remorse. He came to her with a heavy sigh. "My dear Vivian, *la mia rosa,* of course it is difficult to do this. You have been queen of my castle for so long. But we must face facts. We are no longer in our youth. Time marches on and we must march with it, yes? Skye is in the bloom, while your petals are…withering. You cannot bear children and I've been thinking it's time to move to the next phase of life. Nico is a good boy, a fine son. A boy such as Nico would do any man proud. Skye would rejoice in another child. I would fill my home with the sounds of my children's laughter. Imagine how wonderful that would be." His eyes shone with delight and she felt something inside her shrivel and die. Her hands curled into tight fists and her fingernails dug into her flesh. But again, Belleni noticed nothing. "And of course, you could be their beloved *nonna*. We could all be one happy family."

She turned away so as not to let him see the rage percolating inside. "I cannot make promises but I will try to find a solution to your problem."

And to her own. She would rather see them all dead than move that scheming whore into this house. She couldn't bear the thought of knowing Belleni was bedding the woman under the same roof on a regular basis. She choked down a shudder of disgust. Belleni was becoming a soft old fool if he thought she'd just roll over and accept whatever he dished out. He had forgotten who has been the glue of this operation for more than twenty years.

It was time to remind him.

CHAPTER THIRTEEN

CHRISTIAN PICKED UP THE PHONE and dialed his brother Thomas for a quick preview of what he could expect from Mama Jo.

"Hey, buddy," Thomas said, picking up the line on the fourth ring, which meant he'd screened the call and almost let it go to voice mail but since he picked up Christian would let him slide. "What's new?"

"I had a great meeting with a possible investor, feels good. I mean I know I've come close before with banks but this feels right."

"I'm happy for you. So what's up?"

"Can't a guy call his brother for a little chit-chat?"

"Sure. Except that's not what we do. Because we're not girls," Thomas said bluntly.

True. "Okay, you got me. Mama Jo called me the other day and it's been a while since I've been home. I know she misses me but I just can't seem to get away, especially right now. I figured, since you're there..."

"Coward."

"Coward? No, I just don't want to get blindsided. A good defense is a good offense, right?"

"Look at you, afraid of a four-foot-ten-inch black woman." He tsked, plainly enjoying Christian squirming and rightly so. "Just call her. She worries about you. I don't know why but she worries more about you in the big bad city than Owen all the way in California fighting liberal tree huggers and me getting shot at. Go figure. Gotta love her, though."

Christian smiled around the love they both felt for their foster mother. "Owen's fighting tree-hugging liberals?" he said, picking up that thread of conversation. "How's that going?"

"Last I heard, not well. I told him he ought to ditch California altogether but the man seems to love it there. Apparently, there's some group trying to shut down his logging operation. It's a mess. But back to you," Thomas said. "She understands why Owen can't visit often but she doesn't understand what keeps you away. And it hurts her feelings when you dodge her calls."

"I didn't dodge them exactly," he said, guilt lodging a rock in his belly. Sending her to voice mail a time or two was not exactly dodging. "But okay, I hear you. So, everything is good with her, though? She's not sick or anything?"

"Sick?" Thomas repeated, concern following confusion. "Why would you say that? Did she say something to you about not feeling well? I mean, she had some tests run but she said they were routine for a woman her age."

"Like what kind of tests?" he asked.

"I didn't ask. She's so private about that stuff. I figured if she had something to tell me she would but now you've got me freaked out."

"Well, you're right about her guarding her private business but maybe we ought to find out what kind of tests she's having done. I'd feel a whole lot better if I knew what was considered routine."

"Yeah, that's a good point," Thomas said, but wasn't about to let Christian off the hook so easily. "Just give her a call, okay?"

"I will," he promised. "And you let me know if you find anything above and beyond routine."

"Deal," Thomas said. "Listen I gotta go. It's good talking with you, kid. Let me know how that club deal works out for you. I'm crossing my fingers that it's what you've been hoping for."

"Take it easy, Thomas."

"You got it. Talk to you later, little brother."

Christian clicked off, a nostalgic smile lifting the corner of his mouth. When they were kids, Thomas had been the one who had been the muscle in the group. In the beginning kids had mistaken Thomas's quiet nature for weakness. They hadn't suffered that illusion long. No one had been surprised Thomas had chosen law enforcement. It was a natural fit. Christian missed him. Hell, he missed home. He'd been pushing away anything that felt like homesickness for weeks, too driven by this pending deal with Frank Rocco to allow anything else to take hold. He glanced at the dark, thunderous clouds rolling in, heralding the spring storm on the way. "So much for a day at the park," he said, sighing. Mathias would be bummed to miss out on a day away from the center. Not to mention some time practicing his batting skills. His phone jumped to life and he saw that Gage was calling. He picked up, hoping it was news from Rocco.

"Yeah?" he answered, trying to stay calm.

"Dude, we are so close I can smell it. Frank had nothing but good things to say about you. You nailed the interview, but then I'm not surprised. There's a reason we call you The Closer. Here's the deal… Frank wants another meeting. A dinner meeting *at his place.* Do you understand the significance of this?" Gage exclaimed, giddy. "Let me tell you—it's huge. We're in. Why else would he call a meeting in his personal space unless he was ready to seal the deal?"

Christian grinned, Gage's enthusiasm contagious. "Yeah? So when does he want to meet?"

"Next Friday. He said he'd call me with the specifics."

"Sounds good. Just let me know as soon as you find out so I can get my shift covered."

"You got it, man," Gage agreed, then added with a grin in his voice, "Hey, you've got a sixth sense about people. How'd you know that I liked Irena when I didn't know myself?"

"I've spent my life watching people. Their body language says what their mouths don't want to tell. Even though your hands were on Madeline, your eyes kept straying to Irena. And when you looked at her, there was a hunger. So, how's it working out for you?"

"Pretty good. She's…damn amazing," he admitted. "But I still can't wrap my brain around it sometimes. I mean, she's not the kind of girl I would normally go for."

"Why? She's funny, smart, beautiful. You don't like those kinds of girls?"

"You know what I mean, man. She's a bit on the healthy side, very curvy."

"In my experience, a woman with soft curves is nice when they're pressed up against you, right?"

"Oh, yeah, very nice."

"So, don't worry who turned your head yesterday when you've got a gorgeous woman in your today."

Gage cracked up. "Look at you going all philosophical. All right, that's about all I can take of that even if it is good advice," he mused. "See you Friday."

"Friday," he confirmed and they both clicked off. Hot damn. This was going to happen. Finally!

SKYE WAS GETTING READY to leave for the dance studio when Vivian walked into the apartment. Skye hated when she did that but knew picking a fight with Vivian at this moment wasn't in her best interests so she simply greeted her with a forced smile. "Good morning, Vivian. What brings you by today?" she asked. "You didn't bring Nico so apparently a visit isn't on the agenda so what is it?"

Vivian, wearing a smart pant and jacket combo that accentuated her long legs and impossibly tight waist, smiled with seeming kindness and somehow that was far more disturbing than when she snarled and hurled insults. Skye understood cruelty and cool, calculating rage from Vivian, not kindness and warm smiles. "Skye, may we talk, woman to woman?" she asked, further startling her.

"About what?" she asked baldly. She couldn't imagine there was anything she'd want to discuss woman to woman with Vivian.

Vivian lowered herself into the sofa, her expression contemplative. "Do you know how long I've known Belleni?" she asked.

"No." And she didn't care. "Why?"

Vivian ignored her query and continued along her own conversation path. "We came from Italy together. We were lovers. My family didn't approve. He came from humble beginnings but he had a fire inside him that drew me and I knew someday he was going to be someone in this world." She allowed a small, satisfied smirk. "I wasn't wrong. I gambled and I won. But all victory comes at a cost." She hesitated and looked away. Against her better judgment, Skye felt herself sucked into Vivian's odd choice of tales for story hour. She hadn't known the history behind Belleni and his pitbull but suddenly a lot of puzzle pieces were sliding into place. "You were not the only one to carry Belleni's child," she said, returning her gaze to Skye, who suffered an all-over body shudder at the revelation.

"You have a child?" she asked, stunned.

"I didn't say that," Vivian corrected her sharply. "I aborted. It was the sensible thing to do and I don't regret it. Belleni wasn't ready to be a father and I certainly wasn't ready to be a mother. Up until recently, I had believed that was the way of things and the way it should be. However, events of late have changed the status quo and it requires a change in plan."

"What are you talking about?" Skye asked, a trickle of dread causing her stomach muscles to clench in alarm. "What events?"

At that Vivian smiled, only this time there was no kindness there. "Belleni has changed his mind about fatherhood," she said. "It would appear that he wants to formally recognize Nico as his son to the world. The story will be that he and I adopted the boy and we will raise him together. Of course, it doesn't make much sense to have you hanging around once we formalize the paperwork for his adoption so it would be best for you to quietly fade away from Nico's life."

A gust of air left her lungs and she gasped against the horror blithely falling from Vivian's lips. Take her son? Over her dead body. "That's not going to happen, Vivian," Skye said, her tone strained, her heartbeat fluttering. "You cannot take my son like it's your right to do so. He is mine. I have rights.

I'll go to the police. I can take you both down with everything I know," she said, tears blinding her.

Vivian chuckled. "Oh, that would be unfortunate on your part. Let's say that you do go to the authorities with some tale of illegal activity going on that sparks an investigation. There is no evidence conveniently lying around aside from your word but I imagine a wealth of evidence proving you've been supporting yourself as a prostitute will surface and you may even see jail time. And when the police discover that Belleni and Nico share DNA, it's doubtful the judge wouldn't see it our way and conclude that it would be best if you did not see the boy. Oh, and I would hate to hear that something dreadful happened to you. Accidents happen all the time to witnesses for the prosecution. New York can be a very rough town, I hear. Women's bodies are found all the time, some never identified, and the crimes never solved. Nasty business."

Skye's hands were shaking. "Why are you doing this? You don't even like Nico," she said.

"He belongs to Belleni and Belleni belongs to me," Vivian said simply. Her expression softened into something akin to compassion as she said, "Don't worry, I will raise him to be a fine son. Far better than you are capable. Besides, the unfortunate truth is that you are a terrible mother."

"I'm a good mother," she disagreed hotly, wishing she could rip every strand of hair from the woman's head but her feet were rooted to the carpet as a sense that none of this could possibly be real kept washing over her. "I'm not having this conversation with you. I'll take up my concerns with Belleni. You can leave now, Vivian."

Vivian rose. "Don't waste your time. You know how Belleni hates to be bothered with trivialities. I've only come to you as a courtesy. This is happening. I've already set the wheels in motion. However, I'm not a cruel woman," she said, causing Skye to gape with incredulity. "I realize you'd probably like to spend a night or two with the boy to offer your goodbyes. I will make this happen for you. As a gesture of kindness and understanding." She smiled, speaking into her phone. "Bring him up, Vincent," she instructed in an even tone. At first, Skye could only stare, the situation spiraling so completely into a nightmare that she couldn't speak but when she found her words again, her voice was choked with tears.

"You can't do this." She started toward Vivian. "You can't."

Vivian's thinly arched brow lifted in sardonic amusement. "Silly twit…it's done. Frankly, I'd have thought you'd be relieved to no longer have to worry about the boy's welfare. You can take solace in the fact that he'll be raised with the best of everything, with every advantage."

"I gave birth to him, not you," she whispered. "I won't walk away from him."

"Always so difficult," Vivian murmured with a

small sigh. Vincent appeared at the door with Nico. Nico looked with uncertainty between the hulking bodyguard and Vivian until Vivian gestured for him to go to his mother. Nico ran into Skye's arms and she clung to her child, unable to believe what was happening. Vivian smiled and checked her watch. "I will return for the boy tomorrow afternoon. Is that sufficient time?" Skye didn't dignify the question with an answer and simply glared. Vivian gave a tinkling little laugh. "Use your time wisely," she suggested and then let herself out with Vincent in tow.

CHAPTER FOURTEEN

SKYE DROPPED TO THE FLOOR, her knees simply giving out on her, and sat there stunned, unsure of what to do.

"Mama?" Nico's worried voice filtered through the haze. "What's wrong?" he asked.

"Everything," she moaned, unable to hide her fear. She gripped his little arms gently. "Baby, I need you to go to your room and pick out a few of your favorite toys, only the ones you can fit in a backpack, okay, sweetheart?"

"Why?" he asked, and she wanted to wipe away that solemn expression that had become much too familiar as of late. "Are we going on a trip?"

"Yes, baby, but we have to leave real soon so go do as I ask," she said, pressing a quick kiss to his sweet forehead. He nodded and went to his room, his easy acquiescence another stab to her heart and further proof that her son was not living a normal life. He was too accustomed to unstable circumstances to question as the average four-year-old would. Not anymore!

Vivian and Belleni thought they were going to steal her child and she was going to just smile and send him off with her blessings? The rotten bastards! It wasn't enough that they owned her? That they relished in making her life a living hell? She scrubbed the tears from her cheeks but she could do nothing to stem the flow. If they took Nico they'd take her soul. She'd never survive such a blow. She'd rather be dead. She leaned forward until her forehead met the carpet and she buried her fingers in the plush fibers and screamed low in the back of her throat. For the past five years they'd held her hostage, refusing to let her go, threatening her, using fear to control her and she'd allowed them to rule her. But they'd gone too far this time. No one, least of all that venomous spider Vivian, was going to take her son. She'd kill them all before that happened.

She stumbled to her feet and wiped her eyes again as she went to splash some cold water on her face. *Get a hold of yourself,* she chastised. They've declared war. She contemplated going to the police as she'd threatened to Vivian but she couldn't rat out Belleni without implicating herself. The courts would take Nico and she'd lose either way. Plus, Belleni was a powerful man, well connected to the right people, and it wouldn't be so hard to make a former, forgotten dancer disappear just like Vivian said.

The choice was clear: she and Nico had to leave. And it's not that she hadn't made this decision years ago or even tried to bolt but now Belleni had her reserve and she was basically penniless. Where would she go? Where would she turn? Her parents knew nothing about the situation she was in and it would mortify their Bible Belt roots to learn the ugly truth of what their daughter had been doing for the past five years. They didn't even know about Nico. The shame of it burned as deeply as her regret. She made herself promise never to tell them about her life after her injury. As far as they knew she was living her life in New York as an administrative secretary, quite happy but extremely busy. She wouldn't subject them to the humiliation they'd suffer if anyone knew.

So that left her with precious little options but she couldn't accept that one-way street.

Christian.

She worried her bottom lip. Would he help her? He had no reason to but she couldn't think of another person who might. Oh, please, Christian… she prayed fervently. If there was ever a moment when she needed his help it was now. If not… No, she wouldn't even think of the consequences of her failure—they were too awful to bear.

THE RAIN FELL IN A MISERABLE torrent that tapered off to a drizzle, drenching everything within minutes and ensuring that no one enjoyed their time outside as they scuttled from one place to the next. But even as Christian was disappointed he couldn't take Mathias out as promised, his thoughts returned to Skye. Not even the weather could dampen his good mood and he wanted to share it. The fact that he automatically thought to share his news with her hit him hard. He didn't know how to deal with it, either. His feelings were still in a twisted jumble from the day spent at the warehouse and while he figured the smart thing to do would be to walk away, he knew he couldn't.

His cell phone rang and he frowned when he saw it was Skye. "I was just thinking about you," he admitted. "Listen, I think I need to talk to you about—"

"Christian, I need your help," Skye cut in, the desperation in her voice commanding his attention quickly.

"What is it? Are you and Nico okay?" he asked.

"I know I'm asking a lot but can I meet you at your place? In about an hour?"

"Of course." He didn't hesitate. "Tell me what's going on and I'll do my best to help you."

"When we get there, I'll tell you. I can't talk just yet. I'll be there in an hour. Thank you, Christian."

And then she was gone.

Worry replaced his personal quandary about his growing feelings for Skye but Christian could do nothing but wait and puzzle at what could have spooked Skye so bad that she'd run straight to him with Nico.

It had to be something bad.

And that worried him a lot more than he wanted to let on. He didn't like the thought of Skye in danger and he certainly didn't like the idea that perhaps Nico was in danger, too.

Well, he'd find out soon enough.

WITHIN THE HOUR SKYE and Nico were knocking on Christian's door, her heart in her mouth and her stomach somewhere near her toes. She clutched Nico's hand, her bag slung over her shoulder, and offered a reassuring smile to her son in spite of her own nerves.

Christian opened the door and ushered them in with a playful ruff of Nico's hair. "Hey, buddy, been eating any hot dogs lately?" he asked, gently taking Skye's bag without being asked, though he did raise a brow in silent question at its heft. She averted her gaze for the moment and he took the cue for which she was grateful. "You wanna watch some TV while I talk with your mom for a few minutes?" Nico nodded and Christian got him settled in front of the television before turning to her, a million questions in his eyes. He gestured toward the kitchen area. "Want something to drink?"

"If you have something stronger than Kool-Aid I'm game. It's been a stressful morning," she said. Her hands were still shaking but she didn't try to hide that fact. It would probably help make her case if he saw just how desperate she felt.

"It's too early for wine, how about a screwdriver?"

"Hey, that's practically a breakfast drink, right?" she joked weakly and he set to making her cocktail. Of course a bartender would have a fully stocked bar. She watched as he went fluidly through the motions of stirring up a whole dose of liquid courage and slid it into her hand. She accepted the glass and took a swallow to brace herself. "Thank you. It's good," she said, daring to meet his gaze finally. She saw true kindness and concern there and hope sprang to life. "I'm just going to come out and say it…I'm in a bit of trouble."

"I think I figured that part out already," he said. "What kind of trouble?"

"It's complicated," she began, wondering where to start and how much to share. Christian had never asked the specifics of her profession—she got the impression he didn't want to know—so she'd never told him. Truthfully, she'd been glad he didn't know. Keeping it separate and in the background made it easier to pretend she was like any other normal woman when she plainly wasn't. "Someone is really angry with me and he wants to take Nico away from me as punishment."

"That's ridiculous. Have you called the police?" Christian asked. "And just who is this someone?"

"It's better that you don't know. Trust me when I say I'm doing you a favor. The less you know, the less danger it puts you in. Already, I'm taking a big risk with your safety by coming to you but I didn't have anywhere else to go."

"And the police?"

She shook her head. "No. They can't help me. He's a very powerful man. The kind who makes people disappear if they get in his way. On the surface, he seems every inch the professional businessman but he has…clandestine operations that are definitely against the law but tying him to the businesses would be tricky. Besides, once an investigation started, I'd be toast."

"Are you saying your boss kills people?"

"I'm saying he could. He's ruthless." She drew a deep, shuddering breath, saying in a small voice, "I know he had one woman beaten and whipped for disobeying him." And Vivian had watched, the sick freak. She'd ignored her screams for mercy, her pleas for it to stop, she'd laughed at her tears. Another shiver followed. "He may look like a gentleman but deep down he's a monster," she finished.

Christian grimaced, pushing his hand through his hair. "Okay, so what do you want to do if calling the cops isn't an option right now?"

"I need to get away for a few days…but I'm short on cash…I know how this sounds. Believe me, I know. I had a healthy bank account but he managed to seize it and now he's in control of my cash."

"How'd you get mixed up with this guy?" Christian asked, clearly baffled given what he knew of her already.

"I was very young and naive," she answered quietly. "I didn't realize what kind of trouble I was getting myself into until it was too late to get out. By then, I was pregnant."

"Is your boss…Nico's father?"

She flinched but managed to shake her head. It was a lie but she couldn't afford honesty at the moment.

She didn't miss the sigh of relief. She decided to ease his mind further with another lie. "Nico's father isn't in our lives."

"Oh, well, I got that impression but I wasn't sure and that's a hard question to ask," he said.

"I understand and I appreciate you not prying too hard. It was a painful period in my life and Nico was the only good thing to come out of it," she said. At least that part was true. "So, will you be able to help me?"

"I'll do what I can. What did you have in mind?" he asked.

"Well, I need to get out of town and I need some cash. Could you loan me some money so that Nico and I could get away?"

His brow furrowed as he contemplated her plea and once again she cursed Belleni for taking all her hard-earned money. Without his interference, she could've been long gone without needing anyone else. Suddenly Christian brightened. "How about this... I've been meaning to take a drive to my hometown of Bridgeport, West Virginia, to see my family for a few days. Why don't you and Nico come with me?"

CHRISTIAN THOUGHT IT was a brilliant plan but judging by the way Skye's face drained, he had to wonder if he'd just royally screwed up. He rushed to fix it. "You don't have to. I just thought a change of scenery might cheer you up and I'm a decent travel companion, I promise. No talk radio or baseball channels the whole ride. Nothing but good music or conversation or complete silence if you prefer that."

She shook her head, and he wasn't sure if that was good or bad. He wanted to help but he couldn't really see himself forking over a wad of cash. For one, chances were good he'd never see her again; second, if he never saw her again the odds of getting paid back were slim and beyond that if he never saw her again, he'd never figure out what was going on in his head when it came to her.

But a road trip would kill two birds with one stone. Besides, he could use a few days of R & R. Realizing she still hadn't answered, he prompted, "What do you say? You, me, Nico and the open road. Lots of snacks and an iPod filled with great traveling music."

"I couldn't infringe on your visit to your family," she said, shaking her head. "We're strangers."

"No one is a stranger to Mama Jo once she meets you. And she has a way with kids. Nico will love her. I promise. She's like the quintessential grandmotherly type. You know, kind yet firm, loves to bake, isn't afraid to slap you silly if you're acting stupid...you know that kind of grandmother type. Except she's my mom."

"Foster mom, you mean."

"Well, technically, that's how it started out but she adopted me and my foster brothers so we belong to her now. No giving us back at this point."

Skye seemed surprised that he could joke so freely

about something that surely had to have been painful at one time. "I don't know…it doesn't seem right."

"It's fine. Actually, I think it's a great idea and all you need to do is say the word and we'll pile into my car—"

She looked astonished. "You have a car?"

"Yeah. It's my baby. A Mustang GT convertible. I keep it stored because there's no need to drive it in the city but I like having the freedom of going where I please. It's an expensive luxury, let me tell you. The storage place charges as much as my loft. But it's worth it."

"A convertible, huh?" She chewed her lip, weighing the options. "Is it safe for Nico?"

"I would never drive recklessly with anyone else, let alone a child in the car. And the car does come fully equipped with seat belts," he added with a slight tease in his tone. Anything to ease the burden he saw dragging on her shoulders. "What do you say? Road trip?"

She looked over at Nico then back at him, a long moment stretching between them before she gave him a tentative nod. "Road trip," she affirmed and he smiled at her apprehension.

"A change of scenery is good," he promised, and she jerked another short nod in agreement.

"Yeah. I hope you're right. But we should get going. I'm not being melodramatic about the situation."

"You got it."

Christian made a few calls to cover his shifts at

Martini, let Gage know where he'd be and then after Skye had let the center know she'd be taking a few days off as well, he started packing. And damn if he wasn't shaking like a leaf in the wind.

He had an ominous feeling lurking in the shadows of his thoughts but he refused to add to Skye's burden at this point. They'd figure out the details later.

CHAPTER FIFTEEN

SKYE SETTLED INTO THE FINE leather interior of the American made muscle car and allowed a smile to follow. Nico was strapped into the back and the top was up because it was still raining cats and dogs but even so the ride was enough to make her temporarily forget the crisis that had sent her running. She couldn't remember the last time she got out of the city and she was almost giddy with excitement.

"Am I impressing you yet?" Christian asked, with a grin that was just this side of adorable. "Because that's why a guy gets a car like this. To get chicks." He waggled his eyebrows and laughter bubbled up from inside her.

"It's not bad. Beats walking that's for sure," she said offhandedly, giggling when he appeared wounded. "I'm kidding. It's a great car and you know it. Somehow I'm not surprised, though. From what I know of you, you like nice things and there's no way you'd drive a busted up junker."

"You're right about that. I can't run a business like that. You got to spend a little money to make money as they say. Presentation goes a long way in making an impression."

His blithe statement reminded her too much of Belleni and put an annoying damper on her enthusiasm but she didn't want Christian to see so she agreed with a smile. "You're right," she said as they pulled onto the freeway. "So tell me about Bridgeport."

"Well, it's about a four-hour drive so it's no hop skip and a jump but with good traffic flow it should be a decent trip. I was born in Richmond but when I was eleven, I moved in with Mama Jo where my brothers Thomas and Owen were already living."

Of course she had to ask the next question. "What happened to your biological parents, if you don't mind me asking?"

"I don't mind the asking but I might not want to tell you and lose that air of mystery I wear so well." He winked and she grinned but she sensed behind the jokes pulsed a raw wound that he would do just about anything to protect. "Ah, so I found myself in the foster care system after my mom died and my dad was killed in prison."

"Your father was killed in prison? Oh, my God, that's awful."

"Yeah, got shanked or something like that while he was serving time for aggravated assault. Before you shed a tear for the guy let me tell you he wasn't up for Father of the Year before that. He was a mean drunk and from what my mom said, he drank more than he worked. He split before I turned one, so him checking out wasn't a big tragedy. But losing my mom was hard."

"What happened?" she asked, drawn by his story. Her own childhood had been fairly stereotypical of a Bible Belt upbringing. She'd gone to church every Sunday with her family, got good grades and focused on her dance. For all intents and purposes, she'd been a very good girl, which made it that much more impossible for her to turn to her parents when she should've. The shame of the past five years would be more than she could bear if she knew her parents shared that burden.

At her query about his mother, Christian frowned and that painful darkness she'd sensed earlier flashed in his expression. He recovered well and shrugged it off as if that part of the story wasn't as interesting. "It's not something I like to talk about," he admitted. "She tried real hard to be a good mom but she didn't always succeed. I gotta give her props for trying, though."

"Was she abusive?" she ventured, almost afraid to know the answer. Her imagination conjured an image of a very young Christian scared and crying and it made her flinch.

"She never hit me," he answered with a quirk of his mouth, which she recognized as his attempt at deflecting.

"There are many types of abuse," she said quietly, of this she was intimately aware. "Emotional, psychological…even neglect is a kind of abuse."

"Yeah." He focused on the road, but she had the feeling he was seeing something else, perhaps reliving a scene from his past. She wondered what she would find if she were able to take a peek. He shook off with a sigh whatever had caused him to slip into silence and said, "Well, you know some people aren't emotionally equipped to be good parents, no matter how hard they try."

"Still, I'm sure you loved your mom and it must've been tough losing her so young..."

His expression remained the same, loose and relaxed, but Skye saw sadness creep into his gaze. She itched to reach out to him, to touch him somehow, to communicate to him that she wished he'd had a better start in life, but then he grinned and shrugged, saying, "That's the hand that I was dealt. I try not to dwell on it. Besides, she did the best she could and that's all you can ask for."

Skye nodded but her thoughts strayed to Nico. It was her hope that he never found out what she did for a living when he was younger, but secrets had their own way of making themselves known and she worried how he'd take it. Would he hate her? Would he look at her in disgust? Skye's heart spasmed with pain at the thought of Nico rejecting her for the mistakes of her past. She swallowed and returned her attention to Christian. His side profile was like a Calvin Klein model's with his angular jaw and dark burn of stubble. He looked rakish yet soft and ready to cuddle at a moment's notice. She sighed and wondered if she'd lost her mind agreeing to this trip. Her head was certainly not screwed on straight enough to think clearly. "Tell me about your brothers," she suggested, glancing back and seeing that Nico had already fallen asleep.

Christian shifted in his seat and changed lanes before answering. "That's easy. Thomas is a federal agent and he's always been the one to follow every rule. He's not exactly a people person but once he lets you in, he's the most generous man you'll ever meet. He's also good to have at your back in a fight because he's fiercely loyal and doesn't let anyone push his family around. He's a real good guy. I'd say I'm probably the closest to Thomas simply because Owen moved to California to operate his logging company. I don't get to see him as often but Owen is what we called the diplomat. He was always trying to smooth over the edges we created. But he's no pushover. He's solid as those trees he's harvesting. I mean, the man is, well, he's great, too. I dunno, I guess I can't say enough good things about them. I love them both and would do anything for them."

Her eyes misted at the open sentiment. How amazing to have such a bond with someone who shared no blood. She had a sister back in Iowa but they'd never been close. Maybe that'd been her fault. She'd been so focused on training for her dance career that she never had time for the little sister in the background. Then when it came time to leave, she realized her sister had grown up without her and they were strangers to one another. So many bad choices. If she could do it over again, she hoped she would've reached out to her sister more. But who knows.

"So why New York?" she asked. "Why not Richmond or Charleston? Somewhere closer to home?"

He shrugged. "I don't think I could go back to Richmond. There are too many memories there and most weren't good. Charleston just didn't have the vibe I was looking for. New York is all about class, art and sophistication. I like that. I love the culture, the opportunity and the people. You get it all." He cast a quick look her way. "And what about you? You came to New York to dance but where'd you come from before that? And why didn't you return?"

She forced a laugh. "Because Iowa had never been a good fit for me. I stuck out like a sore thumb. I'd wanted more than my town could give me and, I guess, like you, the vibe seemed better in the city."

Part of that was true. In the beginning, she'd been seduced by the wealth and privilege that came with being on Belleni's arm. By the time she'd been sucked into the escort business she'd been unable to get out. Oh, she would've run back to Iowa if she'd had the chance. Well, maybe not Iowa, per se, but somewhere far from New York. She was sick of it all. And she wanted Nico to live in a house with a yard, not an apartment.

"Isn't it unusual that your foster mother adopted all three of you?" she asked.

"Very," he answered. "But Mama Jo said she knew

when we walked through her doors that she'd found her true reason for fostering. It was to find us."

"That's so sweet," she murmured, already liking this Mama Jo character if she was as nice as Christian said she was. "Imagine if the world had more people like your Mama Jo."

"I know," he said, sobering. "She's one in a million. And she's a fabulous cook. Wait until she makes her corn bread. It's out of this world. When we were kids we used to fight over who got to eat the last piece. It got so bad that she started making us our own loaves."

"That's bad," Skye agreed, laughing. "You couldn't just agree to let one or the other have the last piece?"

"Nope. That was serious business and she didn't make it often so it was a real treat when she did."

"My mom used to make sweet potato pie. You could smell it baking throughout the whole house. It was my dad's favorite." She paused, allowing a wash of memories to rush over her. Tears pricked her eyes. She'd give anything to enjoy a slice of that pie again. She looked away so that Christian didn't see the shine in her eyes and lifted her finger to rub out the moisture. "I never did learn how to bake or cook. With my dance regime and the strict weight requirements, I never saw the need to learn. It's not like I could eat any of it anyway. I mostly snacked on raw vegetables and some fruit. But every now and again I'd let myself have a bite of something off-limits."

"Like your mom's sweet potato pie?" he asked with a grin.

"Yeah," she mused sadly, letting her head drop back on the headrest. "Like sweet potato pie."

CHRISTIAN PULLED INTO Bridgeport just as the last few rays of sunshine disappeared into the chilly evening. Coming home was always a mixed bag. He loved it—the teasing smell of hickory smoke lingering in the air on summer days from family barbecues, the verdant green canopy of hemlock and elm that set a young boy's imagination on fire as he chased his brothers through the dense old growth—but there was sadness behind all those good times, too, and it was difficult to embrace one without the other.

The first time he walked through Mama Jo's house he'd been a boy locked inside himself, exhausted from fighting a system that was bigger, badder and stronger than one eleven-year-old kid. He'd been through a succession of foster homes and when he'd come to the little house stationed at the end of a country road, he hadn't held high hopes. He'd worn his grief like a shield but he hadn't expected to be loved, instead of pitied; accepted, instead of just tolerated.

He'd never brought anyone home before. It felt good to bring Skye. She was hurting and there was no one better to heal whatever was broken inside of you than Mama Jo.

"We're here," he said softly, rubbing her arm to wake her. "And you're a terrible navigator. You fell asleep for most of the trip," he teased, eliciting a small smile.

"Sorry, I didn't mean to, I just conked out." She twisted to wake Nico. "Wake up, baby. We're here."

"Oh, and I think your phone rang while you were asleep," he offered, and she rustled in her purse until she found her cell. She noted the missed call and who it was from. "Anyone important?" he asked.

"Nope." Her smile seemed false but she didn't elaborate. Then she turned the phone off completely. Probably whoever was threatening to take Nico trying to track her down, he thought darkly. When they got back to the city he planned to have words with that guy. They weren't living in the dark ages, he couldn't treat women that way.

Nico rubbed at his eyes and yawned, his dark hair mussed and standing on end. Oh, God, Mama Jo would love him. Speaking of…the door flew open and the impossibly short form of Mama Jo appeared in the doorway as the porch light clicked on. "There she is," he murmured, smiling. He bounded from the car and rushed the steps to gather her in an effusive hug. Her bones felt frail in his grasp but she chuckled and accepted his hug as if he weren't in fact crushing her. "Mama Jo, are you getting taller?" he asked once he'd set her down. "I swear you're taller than the last time I saw you."

"Oh, go on with you, you know I ain't no taller but I ain't no shorter neither so I figure that's better than something." She reached up to push away a lock of hair from his eyes, her expression warm. "Your hair's too long. You look like one of those hippies. Don't they have barbers over in that fancy New York City? Maybe Old Clark can give you a trim while you visit." She didn't wait for him to answer just moved past him and gestured to the car. "Where's your manners, boy? You gonna let your friends sit in the car till it snows? Come on, bring 'em in out of the cold. Catching your death ain't no way to show a person some hospitality."

"You betcha, Mama," he said, waving Skye and Nico over. "I'll get our stuff in a minute. Come on and meet my favorite girl."

Skye picked up Nico and made her way gingerly through the yard and joined him as they went inside.

A wall of memories assailed him as they always did, clamoring for attention as one piled on another. In his mind, he saw Thomas tearing around the corner with Owen in hot pursuit as they bounded for the open door, headed for the lake on a sultry summer day. They packed nothing but their fishing poles, each bragging that they were going to bring home something for Mama Jo to cook up but they rarely did. Mama Jo had never complained, just chuckled at their tales of how "the biggest fish you ever saw" always seemed to get away.

Fact was, the only one who liked fish was Owen.

But they all liked the idea of being Mama Jo's special boy who brought home dinner.

Mama Jo gave Skye a once-over before gathering an astonished Skye into a short hug. "There's only family here," Mama Jo declared, moving to Nico who was regarding her with open curiosity but no fear. "And who is this handsome young man?"

"I'm Nico," he answered for himself, reaching up to finger a tight gray curl on Mama's head. "Your hair is funny," he said and Skye's eyes widened at his blunt statement.

"Nico, honey, we mustn't be rude. We're guests in Mrs.…"

"No Mrs., just Mama Jo. Never had a husband worth talking about so never thought I should have to lug around his name for all eternity. And don't worry about getting after the boy. Children tell it like it is. I do have funny hair but there's nowhere that says *funny* means ugly so there's no harm done. Now—" she reached out to Nico who slipped his hand into her small brown one "—let's see what we can find in the kitchen to eat." She glanced at Christian with a knowing expression as she said, "And I think I might have some corn bread somewhere around here though Lord knows I ought to make you work for it seeing as you haven't been home in a dog's age."

Christian laughed. "Don't go easy on me now, Mama."

"Don't you worry, I won't," she promised as she went to the cupboard and started taking down plates and handing them to him. "But I just happened to have a few things simmering so get yourself washed up and sit at the table so we can have a proper visit."

Skye looked to Christian with a worried expression as she said, "Please don't go through all this trouble. We can just pick something up, some fast food or something."

She might as well have said, "We'll just cram a cow pie in our mouths," for the look of horror on Mama Jo's face. "Honey, you've got a growing boy here, you can't be feeding him that junk and expect him to grow up to be a strong, strapping man. Trust me, I know something about the feeding of boys. I've raised my share of them, ending with this knucklehead and he's turned out just right, wouldn't you say?"

Skye stammered, clearly worried she'd just offended Mama Jo as she said, "Oh, of course, ma'am. I just don't want to put you out. I'm sure you weren't expecting two extra visitors tonight. And well, Nico is a very picky eater. He hardly eats anything I put in front of him," she finished, distressed.

But Mama Jo just chuckled and drew Nico into the kitchen. "How about you two get cleaned up and Nico can help me in the kitchen. Ain't no boy who can resist what I got cooking tonight," she assured.

"I don't like broccoli," Nico warned just as Christian slipped his hand into Skye's and pulled her away from the kitchen. Like Mama Jo said, she knew a thing or two about raising boys…and their picky palates.

"Are you sure…" Skye said, trailing behind Christian as he led her to the back rooms where his old bedroom used to be. He kept her hand in his and then when he'd gotten her into the small room he'd once shared with Thomas, he closed the door with his foot and pulled her close. As hard as he tried to distract himself, he'd been thinking of this moment since the second he let her go at the warehouse. Her hands slid up his chest, scorching the skin where they touched, and she glanced up at him through a fall of dark lashes. "What are you doing?" she asked in a husky whisper. "Mama Jo is going to know…"

Christian grinned, mischief and mayhem in his tone as one brow lifted playfully. "What? I'm just showing you my childhood bedroom, where I grew up, did my homework and dreamed about beautiful girls. That's not breaking any rules, now is it? However," he added as he brushed a kiss across her awaiting lips and shivered at the contact, "*this* might earn me a stern reprimand."

"You don't want to do this," she reminded him, her chest rising and falling in short, quick movements as she gazed at him. "Things might've been different if I wasn't in the situation I'm in but they're not."

"I know," he said tightly, cursing himself for letting his hormones get the best of him. "I just felt like I needed to do it…that you needed me to do it, too. Was I wrong?"

She stared up at him for a long moment and when she finally answered, he almost heard tears in her voice. "No. You weren't wrong."

"Good," he murmured, relieved. "I thought my radar had stopped working."

"Your radar?" She smiled. "What kind of radar is that?"

He answered with a grin. "My l-ooo-ve radar."

She cracked up and he let her go. The beauty of her laughter rivaled that of her face and he realized he wanted to hear more of it.

"Okay, Casanova," she teased. "Where can I wash up? I'm starved and whatever your Mama Jo is cooking smells pretty damn good."

He pointed her in the direction of the bathroom. She flashed him a grateful smile and disappeared behind a closed door. His eyelids shut as he exhaled a long, pent-up breath. The woman was like a drug.

And damn if he wasn't becoming a junkie.

CHAPTER SIXTEEN

SKYE ESCAPED TO THE TINY bathroom, closing the door behind her. Her back against the wall, she let out a shaky breath as she attempted to force her body to calm down.

She shook out her hands but her hypersensitive nerves were zinging at the memory of Christian's lips on her mouth. She couldn't remember the last time she actually "felt" something for someone else. She'd shut off her sexuality long ago as a protection measure or else she'd have gone crazy. Now, those long forgotten pipes were bursting at the valves from the building pressure. She stared at her toes, wondering what she was doing here, in a stranger's home with a man she hardly knew who made her feel things she wasn't ready for. Bad timing, she thought to herself with a healthy dose of morose self-pity. Christian was a good man and even though it'd been a long time since she'd known one, she recognized it in him right away.

She'd been foolish to run off with him, particularly when he didn't know what he was getting into with her. She knew he enjoyed playing the knight in shining armor but it was her responsibility to set him straight. But she didn't want to.

"I'm a terrible person," she whispered, startling when a knock at the door was followed by Nico's voice.

"Mama, time to eat," his voice chirped from the other side. "And don't forget to wash your hands before you come to the table," he admonished, causing her to smile in spite of everything.

They were here; there wasn't much she could do to change anything tonight so she figured she might as well enjoy the evening. There was plenty of time tomorrow to level with Christian. She stepped toward the sink and ran her hands under the cold water before splashing her face a few times to clear her head.

Yes, that was definitely the best plan.

Tomorrow.

AS HE SAT AT MAMA JO'S SCARRED and worn table, the familiarity washing over him in a pleasant wave, he cursed himself for staying away for too long.

"How've you been, Mama?" he asked between savoring the beef stew in his bowl and breaking off a hunk of corn bread to slather it with butter. "You doing good? How's your health?"

Mama Jo waved away his questions. "Tell me what you've been up to that's kept you so busy you can't come home for a visit? Must be something good."

"Actually, I don't want to jinx anything but my business partner and I may have found a venture capitalist who might be interested in investing in our club."

"Ah, so you're still trying to open a nightclub in the city, eh?" she mused, gaze wavering between happiness and concern. Of course, he understood her reserve; she'd been fairly open in her hope that Christian might want to move home eventually. It wasn't that he was particularly special—she wanted all her boys to find their way back home sooner or later. Though she'd never come out and say anything that wasn't wholly supportive so she appeared happy for him.

"Mama, you need to come out and visit sometime. The city has a lot of art you would enjoy seeing. There's an art gallery in Tribeca featuring the photography of this real up-and-coming African-American artist that I think you would enjoy."

"Oh?" Mama Jo said, spooning some stew. "Maybe I will someday."

Which translated to "doubtful, but I'm going to make the effort to appear interested" and Christian bit back a sigh. "Well, just say the word, Mama, and I'll fly you first class to Manhattan."

"Thank you for offering, Christian. That's right sweet of you—even if it's ridiculous. Me on a first-class plane ride. The idea makes me chuckle. Thomas told me you were doing real well for yourself. I guess he was right. It plain tickles my heart to hear how successful you've become. Now—" She directed her attention toward Skye who seemed wary of Mama, though for the life of him Christian couldn't imagine why. Mama could disarm even the most guarded. "Tell me how you two met."

Skye shared a panicked look with Christian and he jumped in with an answer. "At Central Park. Or more specifically at a hot dog vendor's cart. I'd brought a boy I'm mentoring in the Buddy program out for some fresh air and she was hanging out with Nico."

She flashed her gratitude as Mama Jo's eyes warmed. "You're still working with that program? Bless your heart, boy. I see I did something right."

He laughed. "You know you did. Without your influence I'd hate to think of where I'd have ended up."

"Amen to that," Mama Jo exclaimed playfully. Light chuckles flowed between them as they remembered a different time and he was fully aware that it was because of Mama that he could laugh at all. Mama sobered with an apology to Skye who'd been watching their exchange with something akin to wistfulness and he made a mental note to question her about it later. He wanted to know what caused her to look with longing when she didn't realize he was watching. He had a lot of questions when it came to Skye. A faint frown followed that realization but he didn't let it ruin his evening. To be fair, most times he told himself he didn't want to know details but he was losing that excuse quickly. In fact, the more time he spent with Skye, the more he wanted to know everything.

SKYE FELT LIKE AN INTRUDER, or worse, a voyeur, watching the easy and loving banter between Christian and his adoptive mother. At first she didn't know what to think of the diminutive woman—she still wasn't sure—but one thing she did know, feeling the love flow between them caused a wretched pang of homesickness that she hadn't felt in years. For years she'd pushed away any feelings that resembled longing for home because it didn't do her any good to pine for what she couldn't have.

"Where are you from, child?" Mama Jo inquired of her, causing her to stiffen in reflex but she forced herself to relax, as she had already figured that the older woman had a keen sense of observation and Skye didn't want to set off any bells.

"Originally, a small town in Iowa but I came to New York to dance."

Mama Jo nodded as if confirming it to herself. "I knew it. You have the grace of a dancer. Saw it the moment you stepped from the car. But you don't dance anymore?"

She offered a short, pained smile. "No. A knee injury ended my career."

"A pity." Mama Jo shook her head. "But God has a plan. Trust in that."

Skye didn't know anything about that and she hated that particular platitude but she wouldn't dream of insulting the woman who was offering her and Nico shelter for the evening so she nodded and made no further comment.

Mama Jo didn't seem to notice her withdrawal or if she did, she didn't ask her for details and Skye was grateful. Instead, Mama Jo picked up her bowl and moved to the sink where she started to run the hot water.

Christian jumped to his feet and shooed her away. "You made dinner, so now you go rest your feet. Skye and I will do the dishes," he said and for a minute Skye thought Mama Jo was going to be the one shooing Christian out of the room but she relented with a happy sigh and reminded him to put the leftovers away, too, before ambling from the kitchen into the living room, saying something about a puzzle that needed doing.

Skye helped Nico clear his spot and then the boy rushed to find Mama Jo and see what kind of puzzle might be in progress.

"He loves puzzles," she murmured, handing Christian their bowls to wash. "You know, she's something else. It must've been wonderful growing up here in this house."

He grinned. "It didn't suck."

She laughed, accepting a bowl to dry. "Wow. That's poignant and profound. You ought to write copy for greeting cards."

"Hey, I'm just truthful and to the point."

She lifted the bowl in question and he gestured to the cabinet near the refrigerator. She put it away and returned for another bowl. "So what *was* it like growing up here?" she asked, curious.

Christian shrugged. "What you see is what you get. Three squares a day, home-cooked with vegetables from the garden. We fished in the creek, or Owen fished and Thomas and I mostly did our damndest to keep from scaring off all the fish. We chopped wood when we were angry and when we weren't angry, and we used to have whittling contests."

"Who won?"

"Owen."

"Best fisher and whittler. Hmm, this Owen seems like quite the accomplished guy. What did you excel in?" she teased.

"It's true that Owen was the best outdoorsy guy. I ain't gonna lie but I was the best at reading people."

"Excuse me?"

"I could beat anyone at a card game," he shared with a wink. "And at rock-paper-scissors."

She turned, placed her towel on the counter and then wiped her hands on her jeans before saying with a playful glint in her eye, "Prove it."

"Oh, you don't want to go there," he warned. "I'm freakishly good at this game."

"I'm hearing a whole lot of trash talk but someone's not showing me much action."

Amusement glinted in his eyes and her breath caught as tickly fingers of attraction played a tune on her stomach muscles. "Let's make it interesting," he proposed, leaning against the sink with a grin.

"I'm listening."

"Best two out of three, loser has to share some personal information about themselves."

She faltered, her smile fading. That was a dangerous wager. Too rich for her blood. "How about loser gives the other a shoulder massage," she countered.

"Ah, upping the stakes I see," he said, missing her silent trepidation at his first offer. "I see you and raise that offer with loser has to give a massage while sharing something personal." She frowned, tempted to pull out all together and get back to washing dishes where it was safer but he wasn't about to let her. "C'mon, I'm ready to show you my skills. Who's talking trash now?"

She laughed. "Maybe I just want to protect your frail male ego," she said. "You know how men can be when they fail to live up to their own hype."

He affected a wounded stance but his gaze was warm with mirth. "Touché. Now put up or shut up, gorgeous," he said, one curled palm poised above his flattened, upturned palm.

Well, she was about to find out how good he was at reading people, or more specifically, her.

CHRISTIAN SHOOK HIS HEAD, unable to believe he'd just been bested at his favorite game but it was worth it to see her eyes sparkle with laughter at his surprise.

"Don't feel bad. Everyone has to lose sometime, right?" she teased. She'd never been a gracious winner. Perhaps she should've shared that little tidbit about herself. "Now about that massage..." She pointed at her shoulders and winced for effect. "Be gentle, I'm a little tender right here..."

She started when he made a sudden movement and pulled her into his arms, nuzzling her neck even as she laughed nervously, afraid of what Mama Jo might say if she found them tangled in each other's arms in her kitchen. "You're going to get us in trouble," she whispered, though in truth, she found it thrilling to be wrapped in his arms.

"I like trouble," he murmured, chasing little thrills down her back. "Especially when it looks and feels like you."

She closed her eyes against the wave of desire that stole the strength from her legs. "And what happens when Mama Jo whacks you upside the head with a rolled newspaper for acting like a randy teenager when there's a sink full of dishes that still need washing?" she managed to say, though she wasn't entirely sure how.

A rumble of laughter sounded in his chest and it vibrated through her body. She could spend a lifetime pressed against him like this. Skye allowed one last moment of bliss and then pulled away. "I'm totally serious. You're going to get us kicked out on our butts on the first night and I'm not sleeping in the car," she said.

He stepped away but the teasing smirk on his face didn't entirely fade, which completely crumbled her resolve. "You make a good point," he conceded, returning to the sink and grabbing a soapy bowl. "However, I'd be a liar if I didn't say that having you here makes everything feel different. Like *we're* different. You know?"

She did know and it was tempting but likely to leave them both emotionally ruined and she couldn't afford much more of that kind of damage. Not even for Christian. "But we aren't different. Nothing has changed. We didn't meet at the park, as much as I wish it were so," she said quietly so Mama Jo would not overhear them. "And I saw the disgust in your eyes that night when you were cleaning me up. I've heard the judgment in your tone. I'm not naive. I know how you feel deep down. Even if you aren't willing to admit it."

He started to protest but the effort died when he saw the truth in her eyes. "Skye…I have my reasons…" he started but she rescued him from having to share them.

"We all do. Let's just leave it at that."

Christian braced his hands against the sink's edge and leaned forward, head down. "Shit," he muttered, shaking his head. "Skye—"

"Hey, it's getting kinda serious all of a sudden," she joked shakily, risking a short look his way in the hopes that he followed her lead and moved on.

He shrugged with a sad grin that was altogether too heartrending and she wondered how many women fell for the man's considerable charm. "Just speaking my mind. Wanted to be honest with you," he said.

And when she met his gaze she knew he was the kind of man whose word you could "take to the bank" as her daddy would say. He was being straight with her. And she could give him nothing. Still, she offered him a sweet smile, expressing her feelings in the only way she could and pointed at the soapy bowl. "Duly noted. Now, can we finish the dishes before your hands turns into prunes, rendering them useless for my massage? Oh, that's right…I'm holding you to your bet, Mr. Holt, so you'd better be ready to pay up."

CHAPTER SEVENTEEN

BELLENI WAS BESIDE HIMSELF. Rage, bewilderment, grief—he felt them all.

"Are you sure she's gone?" he demanded to know sharply as Vivian looked up from her desk, signing his name to the payroll checks from his legitimate businesses. "Did you check all the places she frequents?"

"Of course I did," Vivian answered, perfectly calm but there was a tiny glint of satisfaction in her gaze. "Perhaps she'll return. Who knows…you took all her money, how do you suppose she managed to disappear?"

Good question. "What have you turned up?"

She shrugged. "Nothing. It's as if she just packed a bag and left with hardly anything. It's very curious."

"*Curious* isn't the word for it, Vivian," he growled, shoving his hand through his hair. "This doesn't make any sense. Why would she leave now? She is penniless, packing a four-year-old around. She wouldn't do anything to jeopardize Nico's safety, which means either something caused her to act recklessly or she's been seeing someone on the side that I'm unaware of."

"Either scenario sounds entirely plausible," Vivian noted with a faint nod.

"Why aren't you more concerned?" he demanded.

She gave him a mildly annoyed look. "And why should I be concerned? You're the one who overestimates her value, not I. A whore is easily replaced," she said, shrugging.

"She is more than that and you know it. She is the mother of my son. How easily you forget."

"Oh, I haven't forgotten. But let's be real, Belleni, you haven't been a father to that boy, so why should I let the fact that you provided the necessary DNA to create that child move me in any fashion?"

As always, when Vivian strove to make a point, she made sure it jabbed. True, he'd never truly given the boy much thought aside from his use as leverage against Skye but he was starting to see the error in that. Now he was ready to truly be a father. "Things change," he snarled.

"For you. Not me. I continue as I always have, with clarity and precision. A business such as ours does not run itself, Belleni. You've grown soft and lazy in your old age," she chastised.

"Watch yourself," he warned, his temper finding a new source, funneling toward the lithe smartly dressed older woman. "You forget your place."

She hit him with a seething glare and they locked stares for a long moment. He saw more than cool disdain there, he saw something that burned like hatred in her blue eyes and a seed of doubt burrowed into his brain. Vivian made no secret that she hated Skye. But just how far would Vivian go to remove Skye?

"Vivian, did you have something to do with Skye's sudden disappearance?" he asked.

Vivian's slow smirk said volumes even if she merely lifted a shoulder in a negligent shrug. "I can't recall anything of particular importance that might've caused her to react so badly. But she is rather high-strung, so who knows what set her off."

Belleni itched to hit something, his temper reaching a dangerous level. He should've insisted Skye move into the house earlier but he'd been influenced too much by Vivian and her obvious distaste for the younger woman. Now she was gone. He regarded Vivian with growing suspicion. "What did you say to her?" he asked.

She didn't stop in her task. "Whatever are you talking about, Belleni? Really…can this wait? I have checks to write before payroll is finished."

"I want to know what you said to Skye to cause her to bolt."

She chuckled. "I find it amusing that you immediately assume it was something I said when you have given the girl plenty of reasons to hate you. Surely you don't buy the sweet smiles she gives you? The seemingly complacent whore? You're a bigger fool than I imagined if you don't see through her facade. Deep down she hates you. Loathes you even. And with good cause. You've kept her from her family, isolated her from the outside world and leveraged her son for sexual favors. Even for you...that's pretty low."

He gaped, seeing a new side of Vivian. "You lie out of jealousy."

At that Vivian pinned him with a deadly cool glare. "What have I to be jealous of with that simple girl? She has nothing I desire. She is an irritant. Nothing more. However, watching you lower yourself, simpering after her like a lovesick hound is revolting. It's time you picked yourself up and stopped slavering for that spoiled piece of meat."

"You will fix this," he demanded, his voice shaking with the barely contained anger erupting in his body. Suddenly, in spite of himself, he replayed events in his mind, seeing things from the angle Vivian suggested. Where he'd wanted to see devotion, he saw banked revulsion in Skye's eyes; where he wanted to see loyalty and desire, he saw coerced and forced action.

Vivian scoffed. "I'm not a miracle worker, you silly fool. Perhaps you've forgotten how you had her beaten for her deception?" She sighed and straightened the stack of checks for her assistant to pick up later. "Oh, Belleni, you look like you're about to have a heart attack. Calm yourself before you expire on the spot. Think of this as a blessing in disguise—"

He crossed to the desk faster than Vivian expected and she jumped when he slammed his fists on the surface, the force of it scattering pens and pencils and other items to the floor. "You. Will. Fix. This." Belleni stared down Vivian as she shrank away from him, real fear replacing her formerly smug and haughty demeanor. Good. Let her remember what it felt like to be on the other side of his grace. "Your years of service and our history together have earned you a reprieve, but if it were anyone else who dared to do this to me, I'd have ripped out their tongue and fed it to them. You are not above punishment, my darling. Do not push me to such dangerous places again. You will not enjoy the consequences."

He shoved away from the desk, away from her tight-lipped fury and slowly regained control. "I want her back by Sunday. I have big plans to implement and I will not have your petty grievances cause trouble. In fact, it is time for you to find your own place. You have outstayed your welcome. Besides, it wouldn't do to have two mistresses in the home. Skye will take her place by my side as we raise our son together."

He felt nothing even though he knew the words twisted a knife in Vivian's bony backside. The woman was nothing but artfully stretched skin and bones with only her bitterness to keep her heart going. He'd been a fool not to have seen it earlier.

CHOKING DESPAIR AND FURY robbed Vivian of speech but it didn't matter. Belleni had passed judgment—on her!—and the matter was resolved without further need for her input. The man was already walking away, giving her his back as if she were some ordinary servant, here today and forgotten tomorrow.

Find another home? Indeed! The man was insane if he thought she was about to docilely slip out the back door with her belongings in a box like some pink-slipped employee. She'd helped build his empire. She signed his checks, handled the business aspect so that he could live his life as he pleased, dabbling in projects that amused him or causes that tickled his fancy at the moment, and yet he dared to send her packing as if she were of little consequence? It was obvious Belleni had conveniently forgotten who had been his right hand in the most devious of transactions; the one who didn't blink an eye at directives that might've sent a weaker person into a crisis of conscience. He was an ignorant fool to dismiss the woman who had agreed to have life sucked from her body so that nothing hindered their upward climb to their shared goal. She'd had vision whereas Belleni had simply had desire. Without her influence and guiding hand, he would've remained a middle-class pimp with a handful of scraggly girls to offer. His clientele would've been tourists looking for a good time away from home and the occasional businessman. Instead, she'd helped cultivate a secret, exclusive stable of the finest women only the ultrarich could afford. And for all that, this was the thanks she was getting?

Absolutely not. She'd handpicked each Rosa Aurora marble tile for the foyer, overseen each and every stone and timber for the building and kept a watchful eye on the craftsmanship of each room so that no detail went unchecked. *Leave?* The man was slipping into early dementia. She would not leave her home.

She bent to retrieve the fallen items from the floor and when each one had been properly returned to its rightful spot, she breathed a little easier. A level head is what she required for the moment. Ranting and raving would gain her no ground, not with Belleni, and besides, she was above such nonsense. The trick was not to allow anger to rule your head, she chastised herself. Don't get mad...get even, as the saying went.

And Vivian knew a thing or two about getting even.

It was just time to remind Belleni of her true skills.

He wanted Skye. He could have her. In fact, she would do as he demanded and return the miserable maggots to his possession. But it would not be a happy homecoming, she vowed silently.

No. In fact, it might be...deadly.

She smiled tremulously. *That's better.* Having a plan always managed to smooth out the edges.

Now to make some phone calls and find that intolerable woman and her brat.

MORNING SEEMED TO BREAK earlier in the country, Skye thought, squinting at the bright light pouring in through the window of Christian's bedroom. She glanced over at Nico who was still crashed out on the other twin bed, presumably belonging to one of Christian's brothers many years ago.

She could smell coffee filling the cold morning air and she could hear someone moving around in the kitchen. She let her head drop to the pillow as she tried to rouse herself but sleep was clinging to her like cobwebs on a hot summer day. She'd slept well enough considering she rarely slept well at all, but her dreams had been filled with torrid imagery that would've made a porn star blush and so she wasn't feeling entirely rested at all. She rolled to her back and had just flung her arm over her eyes with a soft groan when Christian came in bearing two mugs.

"Rise and shine," he announced softly. She shot him an aggrieved look, taking in his flannel pajamas with a barely concealed snort of laughter and rolled away from him in spite of the enticing aroma of coffee. "Not a morning person I see," he observed.

"Very astute of you," she said, yawning and rubbing her eyes. "Now go away until it's at least 10:00 a.m. But feel free to leave the coffee."

"Sorry, no can do. Full day on the schedule," he said, affecting a regretful tone that she knew was completely false. "Besides, Mama Jo has already been up since five and around here, 7:00 a.m. is sleeping in."

"How dreadful," she muttered, burying her head under the pillow, which he promptly removed. She groaned.

"Drink this," he said, thrusting the mug into her hands. "And become human again."

"Ha-ha," she retorted but she accepted the mug and curled her chilled hands around its heat. "Smells good," she said grudgingly.

"Mama grounds the beans herself as a hobby."

"Of course she does," Skye said with an uncharitable sigh. Mama Jo was not only a saint but an amateur coffee bean enthusiast. The woman probably trains Seeing Eye dogs in her spare time, just for kicks. Egad, that was catty. She sipped the coffee and waited a minute for the caffeine to seep into her bones, awakening each part of her with a jolt. The awareness leached away the surliness and she gave Christian a sheepish glance. "Sorry. So not a morning person," she admitted.

"Noted and filed away. Never approach Skye in the morning without promise of immediate caffeine or run the risk of total annihilation."

She laughed in spite of herself, then said, "I was just kidding about Mama Jo. She's an amazing woman."

He laughed good-naturedly and sipped his own

coffee before saying, "No worries. Now, want to know what we're doing today?"

"Sure," she answered cautiously. "Does it involve heights of any sort? I'm deathly scared of heights. So if you'd like to completely wreck any illusions you have about me being a demure, sweet, docile type… go ahead and take me someplace more than two feet off the ground. I turn into a screaming, panicked lunatic."

He sipped his coffee with open contemplation. "Another good thing to know. But no, no heights to worry about."

"So what are we doing?" she asked.

"Have you ever gone horseback riding?"

She grew up on a farm but her sister had been the horse fan. She'd been too busy dancing to add more to her plate. "No," she answered.

"Good. Then you're in for a treat. My brother Thomas's girl owns a horse stable at her parents' property and we're going to meet them for lunch and then go riding. It'll be great and Nico will love it."

"You ride horses," she mused, not quite able to wrap her head around this country version of the city bartender. "How well?"

"I'm not an expert or anything but I know enough to keep from making an ass out of myself."

She grinned. "And what if I was allergic to horses? What then? What was your backup plan?"

"Are you always this difficult?" he asked.

"Yes." She laughed. "Do you always wear flannel pajamas?"

He lifted his cup with a wink. "Only when I'm visiting Mama Jo. When I'm home I sleep naked."

Her cheeks flared with heat and she murmured into her cup, the early morning fuzzies loosening her tongue in a way she might not have otherwise allowed. "That makes two of us." She grinned when his Adam's apple bobbed, his expression a comical cross between pained and excited.

"Now that wasn't nice," he managed to say before spinning on his heel and disappearing from the room.

"I know," she murmured with a soft chuckle. It felt good to flirt on her own terms, to be in charge of her own sexuality again.

"Breakfast in ten," he called from the other room and she sighed with a smile.

A girl could get used to this, she thought to herself, allowing a finger of heat to curl around her heart and give it a squeeze.

Intoxicating.

CHAPTER EIGHTEEN

CHRISTIAN COULDN'T STOP grinning. He had a beautiful woman by his side, a plan to visit with Thomas and he was standing on the cusp of his dream becoming a reality. If he forgot about the circumstances that brought the most breathtaking woman in the world into his life he could almost say things couldn't get much better.

"So give me a little background on your brother and his girl…" Skye said as they made the drive over to Cassi's former home.

"Thomas and Cassi are soul mates or something," he said, smiling ruefully. "Thomas fell in love with her the very first time he saw her but it took having to arrest her to figure things out between them. They only just got together. It was a long, sad story, but suffice to say, they're damn near inseparable now."

"Sweet…I think," she said, giving him a quizzical glance. "He actually arrested her?"

"Yeah. Thomas is a stickler for the rules and Cassi, at the time, was breaking them. It turned out all right in the end but when Thomas went after her he had no idea that not everything was as it seemed. Cassi's stepfather was a real bad dude. Killed her mother actually," he shared.

"That's awful," she said with a short gasp. "What a terrible thing to have to go through. He's in prison right?"

"Yep."

"At least that's something," she mused. They came around the bend of Cassi's place and Skye's gaze widened when she saw the palatial southern plantation-style home. "Oh, wow," she breathed, turning to stare out the window. "You didn't say she lived in a mansion."

"Oh? Yeah, her parents were loaded. But Cassi was always down-to-earth. She hung out with us more than she stayed here it seemed. But yeah, it's a big place. See the stables over there." He pointed toward the large, beautiful barnlike structure. "And I think there's a tennis court around back somewhere."

They parked and climbed out of the car. Nico slipped his hand into Skye's as they went to the front door. Christian gave the door a knock and it was opened by Thomas who greeted Christian with a tight embrace.

"It's about time you came by. I couldn't believe it when Mama Jo called and said you were coming to town for a surprise visit. Come on in, Cassi is dying to see you." Then he noted Nico and Skye and extended his hand to Skye. "Thomas Bristol, I'm this guy's big brother. Whatever he's told you of me is totally untrue. He always had a tendency to embellish," he said, winking.

Skye looked to Christian who had the grace to roll his eyes and she laughed at their easy nature. "He's said nothing but good things, I assure you."

"Oh, well in that case, everything he's said is true." Thomas grinned and ushered them inside.

The house looked different from what Christian remembered, although he'd only been inside maybe twice, as Cassi's mom hadn't exactly been inviting to the neighborhood kids, particularly those whose parents didn't travel in the same circles.

They found Cassi in the expansive kitchen, finishing the fixings for their lunch and when Cassi saw him, she immediately stopped what she was doing with a squeal and nearly bowled him over for a squeeze herself. "Look at you," she said, pulling back to admire him like a fine painting. "You always were a cutie, even as a kid. Seems nothing has changed. How is it that you've escaped the clutches of some determined woman with her sights set on marrying you?"

He laughed at the thought of being tied down, though his gaze did search out Skye before he realized it. Mildly disconcerted, Christian retorted, "Women in New York have wonderfully short attention spans, which suits me just fine."

Cassi chuckled and turned to Skye. "So nice to meet you. This must be your son, Nico? Mama Jo said he's a good boy and that's coming from a very discerning source so he must be an angel."

Skye smiled, ruffling Nico's jet-black hair with love. "I tend to think so but I'm biased. It's nice to meet you, as well. You have a lovely home."

"Thanks, it was my parents' place and I had thought of selling it but the market tanked and I didn't feel like *giving* it away so I figured we'd keep it for a while longer." She slid a look toward Thomas, adding slyly, "And maybe we might need a little extra room eventually so…who knows?"

Thomas coughed, his cheeks reddening, and used the opportunity to lead them to the table where a full spread of lunch choices awaited. Skye's mouth watered and she realized how hungry she was. She settled Nico beside her and awaited their hosts.

Cassi followed and took her seat beside Thomas in the sunny breakfast nook. The windows were open and a cool breeze filtered through the room, giving it a fresh and rejuvenating feeling. She glanced out the large bay windows and sighed. "Boy, you must get tired of this horrible view," she said, almost dreamily. The view from her apartment was the wall of another building.

"It doesn't suck," Cassi admitted cheerfully. "This was my dad's favorite room because of the view. Okay, disclaimer time—I didn't make any of this food. I have no talent in the kitchen since I grew up with a live-in chef. It will be good, though, because

I've used this catering service before and it went over like gangbusters."

Thomas grinned and leaned over to kiss Cassi. The love that flowed between them caused a pang of yearning in her own heart. She risked a glance at Christian who had begun to dig into the fruit salad with gusto and she wondered if it was true that soul mates were possible. It was easy to make that assumption hearing Thomas and Cassi's story and then seeing them in person but what about the average person? Did she have a soul mate? Had she already met him? Was he sitting across from her eyeing the southern fried chicken like a starving man? She giggled at herself and he looked up. "Don't stand on ceremony, get yourself some of this grub before it gets cold," he advised, eliciting a smile on her part.

As she loaded Nico's plate and then her own, she wondered what life would be like if she had the option of indulging in her desire to test out the soul mate thing with Christian.

Belleni's face popped into her head and she kicked it away. No bad thoughts today. Nothing was going to keep her from having a good day. She deserved it after all she'd been through in the past five years. One day off didn't seem too much to ask. If she allowed thoughts of that nature in her head, she'd have to start thinking of what a terrible mess she was in and that she'd jumped ship without any sort of viable exit plan. She'd have to admit she was screwed in the worst way and that would cause her chest to tighten and panic to follow. So none of that. Today was all about living in the moment. Tomorrow would come soon enough.

FOLLOWING LUNCH, THEY VISITED a bit longer and then went to the stables. Christian was eager to take Skye and Nico on the trail behind the house but as their horses were saddled and Thomas went to lift Nico onto Skye's horse, he balked and started crying.

"What's the matter, little guy?" Christian asked.

"I scared," he said in a small voice. "I don't wanna ride the horse. Too big."

Skye bit her lip, disappointment in her gaze. "We don't have to ride the horses, sweetheart. We can do something else if you want."

Christian agreed, not wanting to scare the boy further, but he felt the same letdown as Skye. Thomas, catching Christian's gaze, jumped in to save the day.

"Hey, how about this…Cassi and I were planning to take a ride into town to pick up some ice cream, would you like to come with us?"

Nico lit up at the prospect of ice cream but he looked to Skye first. "Can I, Mama? I'll be good. I promise. Please, please, please."

Skye looked at Thomas and Cassi, uncertain of what to do and Christian didn't want to pressure her so he just waited for her decision but he couldn't say he wasn't sending a silent prayer that she'd agree.

"Are you sure it's okay?" she asked Thomas.

"It's good practice," Cassi interjected, grinning at his brother and he almost laughed at Thomas's expression. It was somewhere between willing to do anything for Cassi and fear at becoming a father. Not that Christian was worried. Thomas would make a great dad. He just had some personal demons to work over before he could take that step with confidence. Christian knew without a doubt he was going to be an uncle soon given how Cassi was pushing. And he liked the idea. Kids were great. He even wanted a few of his own eventually.

"Well, if you're sure," Skye said, delighting in her son's happiness over such a small thing. "Promise you'll be good and you'll remember your manners?"

"Yes, Mama," Nico promised fervently.

"All right," she said, and then added to Thomas and Cassi, "Thank you so much. This is very kind of you."

"No problem. We're going to have fun," Cassi said, extending her hand to Nico who eagerly slipped his hand into hers. "When you return just pass the horses over to the groom and he'll take care of them for you."

"Thanks," Skye said, watching as they left the barn with her son in tow. He could tell she rarely did something like this and it wasn't easy for her. It only cemented his belief that she was an amazing mother. Unfortunately, it also made him wonder who

Nico's father was and why he wasn't in the picture any longer. Hopefully, he'd get the answer to that question and a few more running around in his head before long.

"Let's get going, the sun will be gone if we wait much longer," he said, helping Skye into her saddle and ensuring she was secure and ready before swinging onto his own horse. He gave her some pointers and then they took the horses out of the enclosure and onto the trail.

The trail meandered in an easy loop through a canopy of green, leafy trees and curved alongside a creek that was quite swollen and moving swiftly due to the recent storms. The sound, coupled with the natural calls of the birds, made for a peaceful ambiance that immediately soothed the ragged edges created by living fast and hard in the city.

"I've missed this," he admitted wistfully, drawing in a deep breath of the pine-scented air. "Not the horseback riding, per se, but this place. Home. I love the city, don't get me wrong but there's nothing like the place where you grew up."

"It's a beautiful place," she agreed, an appreciative smile wreathing her face as she surveyed the area, delighting in the tiny, early wildflowers popping from the earth in their eagerness for sunshine.

"You moved as far from the Bible Belt as possible, to Manhattan to dance, right?" he said, remembering the small detail from a previous conversation.

"Yes, that's right," she confirmed, though her lips

had compressed. There was something she didn't want to share. He figured it had something to do with how she ended up as an escort. Well, everyone had skeletons, so he wouldn't press too hard on that nerve just yet. Besides, he had her talking and that was something. She parceled out information like a miser with money and her reluctance to share only fired up his need for more.

"So aside from dance, what did you enjoy doing?"

She sighed, frowning slightly as she considered the question, then answered with a shrug, "I was pretty focused. Obsessive even about making it to be a prima ballerina. Although my sophomore year in high school I was named Corn Queen for the Harvest Festival. I remember thinking at the time it was a big deal. Now it seems kind of silly."

"Not silly at all. I think it's still cool. And since it's confession time, I was named Prom King my senior year."

She laughed. "That doesn't surprise me at all. You have the kind of looks that stop girls in their tracks. You probably broke a lot of hearts throughout your high school career."

"I hope not," he murmured with a self-deprecating grin. "I never took myself that seriously and I really hate being labeled. I went out of my way to be uncool but it backfired and suddenly I was cooler than before."

She cocked her head at him. “How exactly does one go about being uncool, I wonder?”

“Oh, well, in my case I purposefully didn’t wash my hair for a week and wore the same clothes every day, then I found this perfectly awful bowler hat in a thrift store and wore it to school, too.”

“A bowler hat?”

“Yeah.”

“I see how that could totally ruin your street cred.”

He barked a short laugh. “The next thing I know guys are walking around with their version of the funky hat. Some pulled it off better than others. I never set out to be a trendsetter but it happened anyway so I just stopped resisting it.”

“You poor thing,” she said, fighting laughter. “Forced into coolness. The horror.”

“Listen to you, Corn Queen, I know you probably took your share of hearts, too.”

She shrugged. “Maybe. I was too busy dancing to pay attention.”

“No high school boyfriend?”

“I didn’t say that,” she answered coyly.

“Ohh, the lady of mystery returns. Okay, so what was his name and what made you turn your head his way?”

“It was a long time ago, I hardly remember.”

He wasn’t buying that line of bull. “I happen to have it on good authority that girls always remember their first crush, their first kiss and all sorts of other firsts. So out with it, if you please."

"Nosey." She sniffed playfully before relenting. "If you must know, his name was Bobby and I first noticed him in English class. He was a football player and so I hardly paid attention at first but then I saw him totally immersed in a book that wasn't required reading and it made me wonder what else about him was a contradiction."

His brow arched. "Okay, you were way more mature than me at that age. I expected you to say something like, he had a great ass or something like that."

She bobbed her head in earnest. "Oh, he did have a great ass, and amazing abs and the most—"

"I get the picture," he cut in as she giggled. "I know, I asked. It's my fault for going there." An easy silence followed and Christian was tempted to keep things light for the sake of continuing a great afternoon but as much as he enjoyed the playful banter, there were real questions swirling around in his brain that were becoming more insistent.

"What happened with Nico's father? Why isn't he around?" he asked, holding his breath for an answer. As he expected she withdrew and he wished he'd kept his mouth shut but it was already out there. "I'm sorry if it's a painful situation, I just wondered why anyone would walk away from such a great kid, but equally, why the hell would someone walk away from you?"

SKYE'S GOOD MOOD FADED like sunshine behind a cloud but she tried to keep a neutral expression for appearances. She didn't fault him; he was only asking questions any normal person might ask of someone they were helping out, but she wished they could just skip over all those details and just stick to the stuff that felt good and pure. However, it'd been a long time since she'd lived in a place like that so she drew a deep breath and smiled with a slight shrug. "Things happen and not the way we envision," she answered, hoping her answer would satisfy his curiosity. But it didn't.

"You don't like to talk about it," he observed.

"Not really," she agreed, almost cheerfully. "It's just not a time period in my life that brings me any joy to remember, aside from Nico's birth. He's the best thing that ever happened to me." But the price was steep, she added privately. She couldn't imagine life without Nico but sometimes she felt crippled by the weight of her choices. "And besides, like I said, Nico's father isn't in his life so what's the point of talking about it?"

"But Nico's father has a responsibility to the child he created," Christian insisted, refusing to let it go. "He doesn't pay you child support at the very least?"

"Christian, I can support my child just fine. I don't need him. I'd rather do it on my own than have him interfering anyway," she said, only partly lying. "Please, can we talk about something else?"

"Not yet. Why doesn't Nico live with you?" he asked.

"Christian...please."

His mouth tightened as his gaze darted away, clearly unhappy with her request but he was too much of a good guy to press her when she'd given him the back-off signal. She appreciated that about him. She wished she could tell him the truth of things but they didn't know each other well enough for her to even consider burdening him with her problems. Her problems were too much for her to bear—she couldn't expect someone else to willingly shoulder them.

Which begged the question... What the hell was she going to do? She was very nearly penniless. The amount in her bank account would only pay for food for about a week before she ran out.

"I've ruined the mood," he said with a grimace.

"No, they were legitimate questions," she said. "I might ask the same if I were you."

He nodded and although his mouth had lost some of its tension, she could almost hear the questions running through his head at her evasion. They came upon a grassy clearing where the creek widened out and he slowed his horse before swinging down and tying the mare to a tree. "Let's rest a minute," he suggested, stretching his back before coming to help her from her horse.

"Sounds good," she said, grateful. Her thighs were beginning to ache from the unaccustomed position. She twisted her back and stretched, gazing past the glinting waters of the creek to the lush, verdant foliage beyond. "This place is breathtaking," she admitted, soaking up the beauty to remember later. "Everything is so green and alive. When I moved to New York I remember being overwhelmed by the sheer number of buildings everywhere. It was a real concrete jungle and something I wasn't used to. Central Park is beautiful in its own way but it's not the same."

"Yeah, I agree," he said, his voice wistful.

She turned her gaze to him. "If you miss home so much why do you stay away?" she asked.

He smiled, saying, "You sound just like Mama Jo."

"It's a fair question, right?"

Christian nodded. "Sure. I do love it here. A piece of my heart always stays behind when I leave, but Bridgeport is a little too sleepy for me in the long run. I want to own an upscale nightclub. I can't really do that successfully here. And—" He paused, as if afraid to reveal this part of himself to someone. She held her breath, desperately wanting to catch a glimpse of that private place even if she wasn't willing to reciprocrate. "It's hard for me to stay still too long."

"Still?"

He chewed his bottom lip in a distinctly vulnerable gesture, his gaze stretching out to see events from his childhood only he could remember. "My biological mom…she had problems."

She assumed so given he was raised by a foster

mother but Skye simply nodded in understanding, hoping he would continue. She was irresistibly drawn to this side of Christian, where he dropped the mask of the mischievous joker.

"Like I said earlier, she tried," he said, almost defensively before continuing with a sigh. "But she wasn't the best mother. We moved around a lot, stayed in seedy motels most of the time. Or slept on friends' couches. I can't remember a time when we had our own place. School was hard but I was smart so I managed to keep up but…it was a struggle."

"I'm sorry," she murmured, remembering her own childhood and how she'd taken for granted simple things such as a soft bed and security. "So, what did your mom do for a living?" she asked, guessing he'd say something like waitress or maid. The hesitation in his gaze struck a chord. He was ashamed, she realized. She tried to soften his fear. "I'm sure she loved you very much no matter what she did."

"She was a prostitute and a drug addict."

Christian's quiet admission sucked the air from her lungs. She hadn't expected that answer and the shock of it nearly caused her to lose her composure. A pain so fresh and cruel it nearly drove her to her knees made her heart beat harder at the thought of Nico saying that to a woman someday. Momentarily stunned, she couldn't answer quick enough. He searched her gaze. "Now you know why…my head is a mess when it comes to you."

Yes. She understood. But it didn't lessen the shock

or the heartache from the knowledge that their pasts would always be an issue no matter if she managed to break away from Belleni for good.

"When you're a kid, you love your parents even if they're not great. That's how it was with my mom. There were times when she was loving and funny. And I tried to remember those times when she wasn't."

She pictured a young, bereft Christian, lost in the world without his only family and sorrow for him replaced her own heartache. "How'd she die?"

He didn't answer right away, glancing toward the horses where they ripped at the fresh green grass sprouting from the soft ground and chuckled mirthlessly. "We were staying at some old, rent-by-the-hour motel. The place was disgusting but at least the door had a good lock and the beds were relatively clean. I woke up to get ready for school and saw my mom slumped over in the bed next to me. The needle was still stuck in her arm."

"Your mom died of a drug overdose," she surmised.

He nodded. "Heroin."

"Oh, God, Christian, that's horrible. How awful for you."

"It's frightening how easily kids adapt," he said, almost conversationally, as if removed. "The prostitution, the drug use, the transient nature of our lives, it was all normal to me. It was just our life. I never really considered the idea that it might kill her. And then it did. My life was never the same after that. I was scared to tell anyone at first. I just left the motel and wandered the streets, eating from the garbage can at school because I didn't have any money and I was starving. A teacher caught me digging for something to eat and it was discovered what had happened to my mom."

"That's when you came to Mama Jo?"

"Oh, no, I spent a year in foster care before I found my way into her home. I was beaten, starved, kicked around, touched…more bad stuff happened to me in the one year of foster care than my entire life with my mom. By the time I came to Mama, I was pretty messed up."

"Wow," she breathed out. "I can only imagine."

"Mama Jo helped make me human again."

She swallowed the lump growing in her throat. Such tragedy hidden by that disarming, dimpled grin. She'd never have imagined, which was likely the point. She suspected that Christian didn't share that part of his life with anyone aside from who was in his tight circle. It warmed her heart that he'd trusted her with his story. Moisture gathered in the corners of her eyes again, only this time for a different reason.

She went to him and gently clasped her hands around his, allowing him to draw her into the enclosure of his arms. She didn't know what to say, or how to say what she felt in her heart. It was all too fresh and raw to even put into words but she felt something and it was profound.

She met his stare and he answered what was in her eyes with a slow brush of his lips against hers. The sweetness nearly broke her into a million pieces.

CHAPTER NINETEEN

THE SUN WAS SINKING FAST and by the time they returned to the house, it was all but gone. Skye hurried inside, concerned about leaving Nico so long with strangers but she needn't have worried. Her son was having a grand time playing dominoes with Thomas, setting the tiles up to knock them down again with a peal of laughter. His eyes lit up when he saw her.

"I'm learning how to play dominoes," he exclaimed with four-year-old enthusiasm. "What took you so long? I was waiting for a long time."

"We went a little farther down the trail than we had planned. Sorry, sweetheart. We didn't mean to worry you."

"I wasn't worried. I just wondered is all. Can we get dominoes when we go home?"

"Sure, honey. Why don't you help Thomas clean up so we get back to Mama Jo's. It's probably dinnertime." Nico ran to help put the dominoes away and Skye thanked Cassi and offered an apology but Cassi waved it away.

"That kid is awesome. If all our kids are that great, I think we'll have ten," Cassi said, eliciting a short laugh from Thomas. "No seriously, he was great. You're doing a good job."

Skye accepted the unexpected praise and held it to her heart. She'd never heard anything but criticism from Vivian about her parenting skills and it felt good to hear that she was doing something right. "Thank you," she replied, then added impulsively, "I think you're going to make a great mother, too."

Cassi grinned. "I hope so. Thanks." They walked to the door and as they were leaving, Cassi looked meaningfully at both Christian and Skye and said, "Don't be strangers, okay? You're welcome anytime."

They said some more goodbyes and then climbed into the car. Nico yawned loudly and Skye knew right away he wouldn't make it out of the driveway before crashing. Chances were he'd miss dinner but that was okay. He'd had a great day and no doubt Mama Jo would have a full spread for breakfast. She settled into the seat and allowed herself a smile as they pulled away.

"WHAT THE HELL..."

Christian's puzzled expletive drew her gaze from the passing scenery to the driveway where a long, sleek black limousine was parked.

Skye's fingers dug into the leather seat as panic followed.

"Who could that be?" Christian asked, mostly to himself, though Skye already knew the answer and her stomach was churning from fear. She didn't respond but the urge to scream "keep driving" ran through her mind. She turned wide eyes to Christian, her mouth dry but he was already stepping out of the car, concern for Mama Jo overriding all else. She had no choice but to grab Nico and follow, though her instincts were telling her to run like hell.

Skye entered the house behind Christian and barely swallowed her gasp of dismay as she saw Vivian, wearing an ice-blue skirt and matching blouse, perched on a chair chatting politely with Mama Jo. She turned when they entered and fixed a chilly smile on her face. "Skye, so good to have found you," she said.

Mama Jo looked to Christian and Skye, a bewildered expression on her face. "This here lady says you're family. Is that true?" she asked of Skye.

Family? Never. Vivian sensed her balking and moved in swiftly, saying, "Yes, Auntie Vivian. We're quite close. I'd say there's no one who knows Skye better than me. I know all her secrets," she added with a slight chuckle that caused the blood to drain from Skye's cheeks.

"What are you doing here, *Auntie Viv?*" she asked from numb lips. *More important, how did you find me?*

"You didn't answer your cell and I was worried," she answered. "It's a good thing we have the GPS tracker on the *family* plan, otherwise I never would have found you in time."

Her mind flew to the phone in her purse and she cursed her own stupidity. “In time for what, Viv?” she asked.

“Darling, you must’ve forgotten…your uncle is paying you to assist him in a business thing tomorrow night. You know how he gets when he doesn’t get his way. *Dreadful.* Sorry to cut your little trip short, darling, but you have commitments I must insist that you fulfill.”

“I thought you said all your family was in Iowa?” Christian said.

“Yes, all but my aunt and uncle,” she answered lamely, sending a quick hatred-filled glance Vivian’s way, which she simply accepted with a patronizing smile. “Surely my uncle would understand if I wanted to stay?”

Vivian’s gaze narrowed to a pinpoint. “No. He would not. Pack your bags, Skye. We need to leave within the next fifteen minutes.” She stood and thanked Mama Jo for her hospitality, then made her way on spindly heels out the door and disappeared into the dark confines of the car.

“I don’t wanna go,” wailed Nico as soon as Vivian was out of earshot. He scuttled to Skye and clung to her leg. “She’s mean and she pinches,” he said, tears welling in his eyes. “Please, Mama…can’t we stay here? I like it better. Thomas is going to teach me checkers next and I want to stay!”

She gathered Nico in her arms and she stared helplessly at Christian, words failing her. “I’m sorry,” she said, despair blotting out everything from her mind. There was no telling what Belleni would do to her when she returned. A beating was likely. She shuddered and clutched Nico to her tightly. "I'm so sorry…I—" tears filled her eyes "—I had a great time. Thank you…for everything."

"Skye, wait…" he called out, following her but she was already grabbing her bag and heading for the door. "Wait a minute. Let's talk this out. What's going on?" he demanded when she refused to look at him for fear of showing him just how terrified she was. She didn't want Christian's family to be touched by the ugliness that was associated with Belleni and she didn't know what Belleni would do to Christian or Mama Jo if she resisted. So, she ignored his confusion and dutifully climbed into the limousine, tears blinding her by the time the door shut behind her.

"Skye…"

His muffled voice faded as they pulled away.

She clung to Nico who had gone quiet in the presence of Vivian. She stroked his hair and tried to reassure him but in truth, she was shaking.

All semblance of warmth fled from Vivian's face as she said to the driver, "Get us the hell out of this sinkhole of poverty before it swallows us whole." Then she fixed her gaze on Skye, her mouth pursing but it was a long, terrifying moment fraught with building tension before she said with a short, dark cackle, "Belleni is quite angry with you."

"It was just a trip with a friend. I was going to

come ba—" she began but Vivian cut her short with a glance.

"Don't try my patience. You ran because of what I shared with you. When are you going to learn that you are not in control in this situation? However, your recent actions have caused Belleni to reconsider his plan." Vivian cut Skye a short glance. "You're a difficult woman, but you made your bed and you will lie in it. If I were to offer you a bit of advice, I'd say keep your head down and your infernal mouth shut, but then you've never been any good at listening to advice, so why should I bother?"

Sky blinked back tears, overwhelmed by the dread twisting her insides in knots, but she remained quiet in the hope that her apparent contrition might gain her favor. It was a long shot but Skye didn't have much more to hope for.

"You're probably wondering what will happen now," Vivian correctly assumed. Skye nodded and Vivian smirked, exploiting every last moment of power she had over Skye. "Well, it's not for me to say. At the very least, a beating most likely, however, Belleni has need of your services. Stay focused on that for the time being and don't bother pestering him with your false apologies for it will only serve to anger him further," she said coolly, sliding into business mode as if their conversation were completely natural.

"He is entertaining a business client and he would like you to be available as his escort. You will be playing the part of his fiancée. He will expect you to be suitably affectionate but not vulgar. Your regular rate will be waived given your recent behavior and perhaps until Belleni finds a more appropriate punishment."

Although she'd told herself to remain quiet, her protests burst from her mouth, as a near sense of hysteria threatened to steal her ability to think straight. "You can't do this to me anymore," she cried, tightening her arms around Nico when he'd begun to shake. "I'm a person, I don't belong to Belleni and I can't—"

"You can and you will," Vivian cut in sharply. "Belleni is Nico's father. More importantly, he wants a life with the boy *as* his father."

The blood drained from Skye's cheeks as the plain truth of Nico's paternity was thrown out there without warning. Vivian smiled, knowing the impact of her words.

"And if I refuse?"

"Don't be ridiculous. What Belleni wants, he gets. You know that."

Yes, she knew that well. "Why me?" she asked dully, not quite expecting an answer but she got one anyway.

"I don't know," Vivian answered truthfully, a trace of sadness in her tone. "I wish I knew. Once, I thought I knew him better than anyone but I seem to have lost my touch. Among other things." Vivian plucked at an invisible piece of lint on her skirt. "He is a stranger to me now." She drew a deep breath as if fortifying herself and forged on, that damnable mask of ice sliding back into place. "But I've accepted that I won't ever understand and I've moved on. Now, let's get to business. Your clothes have been moved to Belleni's bedroom and Nico's things have been relocated to a bedroom near the pool."

That startled Skye out of her stupor. "What? Why? What about my place?"

"Plans change. Belleni no longer sees the benefit of keeping you in the apartment."

Perspiration dampened her underarms, trying to fathom what was happening. She struggled to keep the horror from her voice at the thought of living full-time with Belleni. "But why move Nico downstairs? He can't be that far from me. He's not even five yet."

Vivian smiled. "Well, it's only temporary, I assure you. We've arranged for an early enrollment at Excelsior. Isn't that wonderful?"

Skye was going to vomit.

Hopefully it landed all over Vivian's expensive shoes.

CHRISTIAN COUGHED AS the limousine spat out a cloud of dust in its wake, still unable to quite comprehend what had just happened. One minute he was having the best day of his damn life and then the next he was watching as Skye allowed that woman—he wasn't convinced that they were truly related—hustle her into the car to drive away.

He swore under his breath, not sure what to do. Should he chase after her? No, he answered himself in the next breath, shaking his head in bewilderment. It's not like she didn't have a choice. She could've flat out told her aunt no, well, she sort of tried, but she could've been a bit more firm about it, he reasoned, trying to make sense out of what was shaping up to be nonsense in his head. Things like this didn't happen in real life. At least not in his. The bottom line was she'd left him behind. He drew a deep breath and slowly walked into the house.

"Christian, what was that all about?" Mama Jo asked, her expression filled with concern. "I didn't like that woman. She had mean eyes. Even when she was smiling. I felt like I was staring down the barrel of a gun with it cocked and ready. Did you notice that?"

"Well, Skye left with her so she must not have been that bad. I don't know, Mama, I'm as lost as you about the whole thing."

"I don't buy it, son. Skye seemed off, like she was trying to hide something and if that isn't enough to make you wonder, her boy was downright terrified. No, I don't like it at all. I think something bad was going on between those two. Bad blood at the very least."

He shrugged, feeling helpless. "Maybe, but there's nothing I can do about it now. She's gone. I'll try to catch her on Monday or if not Monday, then Friday when she teaches her dance class."

Mama Jo's eyes narrowed with worry. "You can't try to find her sooner?"

"Mama, we're not even dating. We're…" Not exactly friends but not attached, either. He finished with another shrug. "I don't know what we are but I don't have the right to go chasing after her when she plainly had the option to stay."

"Oh, pooh on that. I seen the way you look at her and you never would've brought her here to meet your family if she was just a fly-by-night acquaintance. I may be old but I'm not stupid. You're a good-looking man and I don't doubt that you have your share of pretty ladies on your arm but you've never brought one home. That says plenty to me."

He wasn't going to argue. Mama Jo saw right through him and she was right anyway. Skye was special. "Be that as it may, she made her choice and I'll just have to wait to figure things out. I have a business meeting tomorrow night anyway, maybe this is just as well. I don't need to be distracted right now. I need to focus."

"This about your nightclub?"

He nodded. "Best shot I've ever had to get the club up and running. I can feel it."

Mama Jo drew a short breath as she regarded him with love. "I want you to be happy. I wish happiness for all my boys and I know you have your heart set on this club business. All I ask is that you're plenty sure of what you're going after and the reasons why. Fame and fortune never brought no one happiness and you know I've never understood your dream of owning a place where sin and vice go hand in hand but I never said nothing because you seemed set on it. But I seen the way you look at Skye and her boy. There might be a real future there."

"Mama, it's too soon to have that conversation." But her words had already begun to worm their way into his brain, planting little seeds of doubt. He pushed them away. "I don't know what's going to happen with Skye—there's stuff going on with her that's not my place to share—but I've wanted to open a club since I was seventeen and I'm finally at a place in my life where I can make that happen. I'm not walking away from it."

Mama Jo lifted her hands in surrender. "Not asking you to, son. Just talking out loud is all."

He nodded but his thoughts were in a tangle. He needed to get his head on straight. Maybe the open road was a good idea after all. He could be home by midnight. As if sensing his thoughts, Mama Jo chuckled and raised on her toes to kiss his cheek. "It was great to see you. Take care, love, and don't be a stranger. Drive safely and good luck with your meeting."

He kissed her back and lifted her in a tight hug. One thing was for sure, he loved this little woman right in front of him. "Thanks for the hospitality, Mama. Hey, that reminds me, Thomas said something about you having tests? Is there something I should know about?"

"Only if it's your interest to know just how quickly this old body is falling apart," she teased. "Like I told your brother, they're just routine tests. Blood work and whatnot."

"Yeah, but what prompted the need for tests?"

She waved him off. "You've got enough on your plate you don't need a spoonful of what's going on with me. When there's news to tell, rest assured I'll be sharing it. Until then, mind your business."

In other words, back off. He could read between the lines. "Promise you'll let us know?" he pressed.

"As soon as there's a need. Absolutely."

That wasn't exactly the assurance he was looking for but he'd take it. "All right, I'll call in a few days."

"Go on with you," she said, shooing him off, then returning to her chair and tucking her legs under a lap blanket. "I'll hear from you when I hear."

He grinned and went to collect his stuff for the drive home.

CHAPTER TWENTY

BELLENI FIDGETED WITH HIS TIE as the simple task seemed to elude him. His mind was traveling and he couldn't focus. Perhaps he'd been too harsh with Skye. How does one treat the woman he planned to marry? Marry? The word slipped from his thoughts and startled him. He hadn't imagined that he would marry the woman but suddenly it made sense. Why not make it official? They shared a child. It would simplify things by half. She would no longer feel compelled to find a life outside of his sphere and he could take her out of the rotation without fear of losing her completely.

Perhaps they should have another child right away.

He smiled nervously at the thought. Of course, Vivian's strident voice cut into his thoughts as he entertained the burgeoning fantasy.

"She hates you. Have you forgotten that one simple fact? Of course you have, you doddering fool."

He winced. He could rectify that. He would lavish her with gifts and whatever her heart desired. Eventually she would come to adore him.

A knock at his door caused him to straighten with

anticipation. "Come in," he commanded, turning to face Skye as she entered.

Her beautiful face was pale from her ordeal and he wished he hadn't had to be so firm in his discipline but she'd broken a cardinal rule and he couldn't let that slide, no matter his love for her. "Darling, you look ravishing," he said warmly, his gaze sliding over each subtle curve of her lean body clad in a cream dress that had cost him a fortune. "That dress becomes you. I knew when I saw it I had to have it for you."

She remained silent, her gaze bouncing away from him but not before he caught the burn of hatred.

"Are you in much pain, my love?" he inquired, searching her body for marks. He'd given specific instructions to his men not to leave marks.

She stiffened and slid her gaze to him. "What does it matter? I'm nothing but your possession, your plaything. As Vivian has informed me on numerous occasions, what I feel doesn't matter."

Vivian. He swallowed a beleaguered sigh. That woman sometimes made more trouble than she was worth. But there was no time for such a conversation at the moment. There was business to discuss. "Has Vivian briefed you on your role tonight?"

"Yes. I am your fiancée. I am to be charming, engaging, witty and complimentary as well as affectionate without being vulgar," she said as if reciting a script without an ounce of passion.

"Yes, that's right," he said gruffly, gesturing for

her to come toward him. Her gaze narrowed as if to say *screw yourself* and his temper flared at her insolence. "Do not push me, Skye," he warned. "I can be a reasonable man but I can be pushed to terrible things." He didn't want this between them. He wanted her to come to him, laughing, her eyes full of genuine joy and adoration, like she once did. He had to remember to woo her with soft words. He swallowed his anger and affected a kind smile. "Come, darling. Let me see a preview of the woman I will marry."

"It's an act you demand of me," she said, her tone deliberately cutting. "I would never be your wife willingly. I would rather die."

"That could be arranged!" he shouted without warning, the anger slipping from his control with her words. But she didn't back down or apologize, instead lifting her chin, daring him to strike her, knowing that if he did, she'd be useless to him tonight. He wouldn't tolerate such a display from the woman of his heart. He crossed to her in a fluid movement that startled her and before she could get away, he gripped a handful of golden hair, mindless of the artful array of curls painstakingly created by the hairdresser he'd paid to pamper her for the evening, and jerked her to him. She yelped as he felt strands ripping from her scalp. "You will be the lady on my arm or you will be nothing," he snarled, twisting harder until tears sprung to her eyes. "Your body will rot somewhere where no one will find you. Nico will be raised without you and I will never allow him to say your name. I will tell him that you abandoned him. He will grow to hate you for your abandonment. I will see to it!" He gave her a little shake and her cries mollified him only slightly. "Do you hear me?"

"Yes," she gasped, clutching at his hand, begging him to turn her loose. "I'm sorry. I—I'll be better," she cried. "Please don't take Nico from me. He's all I have."

Belleni loosened his grip and she sagged away from him but he caught her and pulled her close. "No, darling," he corrected her softly, smoothing her hair as best he could. "You have me. And that's all you'll ever need."

VIVIAN WENT TO THE KITCHEN to survey the progress the catering company was making with the dinner preparations and as she tasted and critiqued the menu, Skye came in, her face obviously swollen from crying and her hair in a mess.

"What is wrong with you?" she asked sharply, irritation washing over her. "You look like hell. The dinner guests are bound to arrive in a half hour. Go fix yourself." She dismissed her with a shake of her head. Skye's eyes watered and Vivian started at the unexpected show of weakness. "What's wrong with you?"

"Why do you hate me so much?" she asked pointedly, in spite of the catering people milling around. "What have I ever done to you, Vivian?"

The catering people paused to stare at the two women, clearly becoming uncomfortable. "Should we..." one asked, gesturing for outside.

"No need," Vivian answered. "Come, Skye, we can have this conversation upstairs while you have your hair and makeup repaired."

She expected Skye to refuse but something of her spirit had flown and she simply nodded listlessly and followed Vivian.

As Skye sat in the chair at the bathroom vanity, Vivian dismissed the hairdresser and began repairing Skye's hair herself, picking up the limp and bruised curls and giving them fresh bounce with a little spray here and there. The woman had been blessed with the hair of an angel, Vivian noted almost in a detached manner. "Why does one woman hate another? The answer is simple enough if you choose to look." She pinned a curl. "A man, of course."

"I don't understand."

She sighed. "Of course you don't because you've always been a stupid girl. I told you I came to this country with Belleni. We started from nothing and built something lasting and strong. And together we built an empire. The women came and went but I was his rock, his true north. Until you came along." She jabbed a pin into place a little too forcefully and Skye jumped as it dug into her skin. "And then, things changed. He wanted you and only you. He was different. I knew I'd lost him."

"I've told you I don't want him," Skye said flatly.

"Well, it doesn't matter because he wants you," she retorted, a hint of the bitterness in her heart seeping through to her tone. She stepped away from Skye to observe her handiwork. Much better, she noted with a critical eye. "But I've come to a realization that if he is determined to have you, I no longer want him. I refuse to accept scraps. It is beneath me." Skye said nothing and it was just as well. Vivian had shared enough. "There. Your hair at least is improved. Freshen your face and come downstairs soon. Do not sit up here and sulk."

"I have no plans to sulk, Vivian," Skye said quietly. "Belleni has made it quite clear as to my role and the consequences of any disobedience."

Vivian wondered what Belleni told her. No matter. None of it mattered after tonight. "Yes, well, be quick about it. The guests should be here soon."

Skye turned away, but not before Vivian caught the sheen of more tears. A tiny, almost nonexistent piece of Vivian took pause at that obvious show of defeat but her own heartache pulsed harder and deeper, shadowing anything else that might've claimed her notice.

Belleni had once told her that he'd never known a woman more single-minded in her focus, more vicious when crossed. He'd said it with admiration and desire.

Vivian toyed with a smile as she descended the

stairs. Tonight, she would remind Belleni what he had obviously forgotten about the woman who had made everything in his life possible.

She would rejoice in the lesson. Even if it made her heart bleed.

CHRISTIAN AND GAGE ARRIVED at the address given to them and Gage, hyped and excited, commented on Christian's obvious quiet. "C'mon, man, this is it. Put your game face on," he demanded, elbowing him for emphasis.

"I'm fine," he assured his friend but in truth he was distracted. He hadn't been able to get ahold of Skye. She hadn't answered any of his calls or text messages and it was starting to worry him. Even worse, Skye had contacted the group home administrator to resign her teaching post. Once he heard that he knew something was up. Skye loved teaching the kids dance. He could see her joy shining through her eyes as she reconnected to her first true love. She wouldn't just walk away, which led him back to the fear that he should've done something more to prevent her from leaving with that dragon woman. He could still see her wide eyes and pale face as she disappeared into the limo. He hadn't taken her seriously enough when she'd said she was being chased by someone really bad. He hadn't imagined that it was as dire as she had made it out to be. And now he was scared that he might've watched her climb right inside the gaping mouth of whoever was trying to eat her alive.

The thought made him nauseous. He swallowed the bile in his throat and made a concentrated effort to focus on the meeting.

A doorman opened the door and ushered them inside the opulent home. Fine furnishings filled the room and expensive art hung on the walls.

"Nice digs, eh?" Gage said under his breath. "Imagine, this could be us someday if things go right."

"Yeah," Christian agreed, though this wasn't what he'd call homey. He certainly couldn't see himself raising a kid in this place. It was like walking through a museum of rich stuff and you couldn't touch anything.

The doorman left them in a sitting room and just as he was about to take a seat, Frank Rocco walked in with a wide smile and a woman on his arm that immediately caused the spit to dry in Christian's mouth and his brain to balk.

"Gentlemen, so good to see you again," Frank said, then patted the small hand curled around his bicep. "May I introduce the woman I will soon have the pleasure of calling my wife, Skye D'Lane."

And then Christian felt the world drop out from under him.

SKYE HAD MUCH THE SAME reaction as Christian but she was much better at hiding it. For his part, Christian actually seemed to stumble a bit before regaining his equilibrium to stare hard in her direction.

Belleni, going by his other name, Frank Rocco, noted Christian's reaction. "Something wrong? Feeling okay?" he asked.

"Fine," Christian answered, cutting his gaze away from Skye. "Had a beer before we came. Must've went straight to my head."

"A bartender who can't hold his liquor? That's a new one," Belleni joked with hearty laughter. "Come now, let's discuss how we're going to meld our futures together in an equally profitable venture."

Gage rubbed his hands together with obvious excitement. "I'm all for that. What do you say, Christian?"

He nodded but his gaze kept straying to her, and she did her best to keep her expression neutral, betraying nothing of the horror she felt from this meeting. She'd never in a million years imagined that Belleni was Christian's benefactor, the man who held the key to his dreams. But now that she gave it some thought it seemed fitting. At first glance Belleni always made it appear as if he were the answer to someone's prayers, the ray of light in a dark room. Until they realized his true nature—and by then they were stuck.

She couldn't let Christian get into bed with Belleni, not when he still had a chance to be free.

Skye tried to catch Christian's gaze but he steadfastly ignored her, while he traded easy banter with Belleni and his friend. Her heart hammered hard against her chest as she ran through possible ways to get him alone before the night's end but Belleni kept her close, taking every opportunity to touch her possessively in some way, making it loud and clear that he knew her body. Her cheeks burned but she did her best to parlay her embarrassment into an act of modesty when in reality she wanted to vomit knowing Christian was forced to watch and pretend he didn't care.

She knew differently. The tension in his jaw was subtle but it was there and she knew what caused it.

"So, how long have you known each other?" Christian inquired politely, though Skye heard a thread of steel in his tone. Gone was the sweet, caring, understanding man she'd known only two days ago. She bit her lip and looked away, knowing Belleni's answer would kill whatever feelings Christian may have had left for her.

Belleni put his hand on her thigh and rubbed the fine silk softly. "Five years. We have a son together. I finally came to my senses and decided to make an honest woman of her," he said, leaning over to steal a kiss but she cheated her face just in time, giving him her cheek instead.

"Sweetheart, our guests don't want to watch us fawn all over each other," she said, swallowing the acid in her throat.

"Of course. I forget myself around you, darling," he said, though his gaze had darkened at her rejection.

"Five years…that's *amazing,*" Christian said,

ignoring his friend Gage's subtle shift at his odd emphasis. He scooted forward, pinning her with a dark, speculative look. "You know, I swear I've seen you somewhere…"

"I doubt that," she murmured, pleading silently for him to drop it. "I don't get out much."

"No, I'm sure of it," he said, snapping his fingers. "I got it. You were a dancer, weren't you?"

She breathed a secret sigh of relief. Her dancing career was safe enough. She allowed a small laugh and said, "Oh yes, but it was a long time ago. I danced with the New York Ballet Company. Perhaps you caught one of my shows?"

"Perhaps," he agreed.

Belleni puffed with pride. "My girl lit up the stage with her talent. That's how we met. I would watch her dance. When I heard of her injury I knew I had to be there for her. And then we fell in love. It was like something out of a storybook."

Christian's expression soured but only by a fraction and Belleni completely missed it, thank God. Skye swallowed and nodded. "Yes, a long time ago. I hardly feel like the same person," she said, hoping against hope that perhaps Christian heard the tiniest message hidden between the lines. "So much has changed."

"Except our love," Belleni added, giving her a short look.

"Of course," she replied quietly in agreement. "Our love."

Vivian entered the room and her eyes alighted on Christian. Recognition flared and she cocked her head slightly to the side as if assessing her next move. Skye held her breath. The entire room seemed to buzz with the growing tension that only Skye could sense.

Christian's eyes narrowed as Vivian smiled at him, daring him to say a word, but he didn't rise to the challenge and Skye was grateful.

"Dinner is served," she announced in a light and softly cultured voice that she reserved for their most important guests. "Skye, would you mind helping me for a moment?" she asked as they filed into the formal dining room.

Belleni lingered. "What is wrong?" he asked. "You look ready to fall to the floor."

"I'm a little light-headed," she said, searching for an excuse. "Probably just hungry."

Belleni's expression softened and he caressed her cheek. "Darling, you mustn't run yourself down like that. Go with Vivian, I will ensure you get plenty of food on your plate when you return."

"Thank you," she murmured with false appreciation and he visibly swelled with pleasure. Skye caught Vivian's lip curl at his reaction and she felt caught in the middle of a deadly game.

Once they were alone, Vivian settled her stare on Skye. "Why didn't you mention that your lover was Belleni's newest pet project?" she demanded.

"I didn't know," she answered truthfully, still

feeling sick to her stomach. She was in hell. "Don't you think I would've steered clear if I'd known? I tried to protect Christian from Belleni. I didn't tell him anything but I wish I had," she added with a hint of venom, her spirit returning. "I wish I'd told him every dirty little secret I've discovered over the years, including a few of yours."

"You truly despise Belleni, don't you?"

"With every fiber in my being."

"And yet you sacrifice everything for the boy who is a part of him," she mused, almost to herself.

"Nico isn't his son. He is separate and a part of *me*."

Vivian seemed to consider Skye's answer. After a long moment she asked a simple question that threw Skye completely.

"If you could walk out the front door without restraint, would you promise to take that miserable boy of yours and never subject me to your wretched face again?"

Skye stared hard at Vivian, trying to discern her game, her twist of cruelty, but she saw something else, something she'd never seen before. It was this glimmer that caused her to answer with a fervent vow. "I would do anything you asked if I could take my son and live without fear of Belleni coming after us."

"*Anything?* Interesting." Then whatever Vivian was thinking was sealed off from her expression and she snapped to business mode. "That will be all. Return to the dining room and put on a good face. Belleni will have his night and I have details to attend."

Confused, Skye returned to the dining room with a gracious smile, much like Vivian's, slipping into a part that she was tasked to play.

Hopefully, the night ended swiftly. She couldn't take the strain much longer.

CHAPTER TWENTY-ONE

CHRISTIAN COULDN'T HELP himself, he'd lost all focus. Anger, raw and mean, swirled through him at Skye's deception. Each time he thought of the lies that she'd spoon-fed him, he wanted to break something. And that was saying a lot because he wasn't the kind of guy who smashed plates and shit when he was mad. But right now, he was in a danger zone.

This was supposed to be the happiest moment in his life and yet he was fuming about a woman he'd known only a handful of weeks. So she lied. Big deal. It's not like he'd been planning to ride off into the sunset with her.

Actually, maybe he had. Eventually. But she'd known all along that wasn't going to happen. She'd played him. A part of him—the rational part likely—tried to remind him that Skye had never given him promises and had almost always shied away from answering personal questions. But he had shared intensely personal things about himself and his childhood—something he never did—with a woman who'd been holding back the whole time with no intention of being honest with him. She'd said Nico's father wasn't in the picture, yet here he was, sitting at the man's table, forced to watch as Skye accepted his kisses and his touch. Was any of it real? Had she ever been in danger? The only thing he knew had been real was that moment he dragged Skye from the Town Car. After that…he couldn't be sure. Rich people played sick games and he should've trusted his instincts to keep his distance from Skye D'Lane.

Dinner traveled at a snail's pace and although he did his part to appear interested, he wanted to get the hell out of there as soon as possible. Gage nudged him under the table when he seemed lackluster and perhaps had started glowering without his realization, and Christian felt bad for the guy. For all Gage knew, Christian was in danger of blowing off the biggest deal ever for no apparent reason but it wasn't like he could break down and explain why he wanted to just leave.

No, he wanted to stomp out of there and tell Frank Rocco thanks but no thanks because he couldn't spend the next couple of years smiling across the table at Skye, without wanting to do or say something inappropriate. He couldn't pretend that he hadn't imagined life with her by *his* side. He wasn't that good an actor.

And it pissed him off that he was going to walk away because of it.

Christian stood, unable to stand another minute, and tossed his linen napkin to the table, shaking his head. "I'm sorry, Mr. Rocco, I've got some bad news," he announced, causing Gage to stare. "I can't do this."

Gage's surprise turned to shock. "What the hell are you doing, man?" he asked in a harsh whisper. "You're screwing us both."

"I know and I'm sorry," he bit out, shooting Skye a dark look. "I'm not the kind of man who can smile and pretend everything is okay when it's not. I wasn't raised that way and I don't intend to start now."

Frank was flabbergasted. "Have I offended you in some way?"

"No. But she has," he said, unable to stop himself. Skye gasped, that pleading look returning to her gaze that he didn't fully understand. "You lied to me."

"Please don't do this," she whispered, causing Frank Rocço to stare at them both. "I'm begging you to stop. There's far more at stake than you realize."

"Yeah, sure. I can see why you were only playing with me. Why give up all this?" He gestured to the lavish surroundings. "This is the jackpot, baby."

"You know him?" Frank grabbed Skye's arm hard enough to leave bruises and Christian started to intervene but the man stopped him with a look. "You stay put, boy. Answer me, you faithless whore!"

Christian's anger at Skye took a distinct turn and he growled at Frank. "Watch it. There's no reason to call her names," he said.

Skye trembled. "Christian, just go. I'm sorry…I wanted to tell you but—" she risked a look at Frank, and Christian saw hatred flash there "—this is the man who threatened to take my son from me."

Gage stood, his face white. "Maybe we should go..."

Christian mentally stumbled from her admission and his gaze flew to the man he'd believed was the answer to all his dreams. "Is this true?" he demanded.

"I don't explain myself to people like you," Frank answered coolly, narrowing his stare at Christian. "The boy is my son. Ask her."

Her mouth tightened but she nodded. "Yes. A fact you've exploited since the day he was born. You're no father to him. You're just a stranger he lives with."

Belleni reacted quickly, slapping her hard across the face, shaking her like a rag doll when she nearly collapsed. "Come any closer and I'll make your life a living hell," he spat in warning when Christian started for him. "Now get out of my house."

"I'm not going anywhere until you take your hands off her," Christian said, his gaze narrowing on Frank. "Now."

"Christian, please," she pleaded, tears welling in her eyes, "just go. He doesn't make idle threats. Get out while you can."

"I'm not going anywhere until I know you're going to be safe," he said. He was still angry as hell but there was no way he was leaving her with Frank when he'd already cracked her in the face. He should've kept his mouth shut and just walked but he hadn't been able to and now Skye was paying the price. He couldn't abide that.

Frank sneered. "Look at you, the whore's champion. How noble."

"What is wrong with you?" he asked incredulously, his temper rising, and his fist clenching. "Stop calling her a whore before I put my fist in your mouth."

"Why should I? It's what she is. She screws men for money. *It is her job,*" he said, letting go of Skye as if she were contaminated and he might catch something. "There have been countless men between her legs. Including me," Frank said with a casualness that was insulting.

"Stop it," Skye sobbed, covering her face with her hands. "Don't do this, please."

Revulsion crowded his thoughts and he wasn't sure if it was directed at Skye or Frank but he knew he couldn't stay any longer without wanting to do some damage. Gage muttered, "You're on your own, pal," and disappeared to escape the ugliness unfolding like a bad movie.

Christian hardly noticed Gage's departure. "Where's Nico?" he asked with a steely calm that shocked Skye. She wiped at her eyes and slid from the chair, away from Frank who was watching Christian with murder in his eyes. "Go get him."

Skye hesitated only a second before fleeing from the room.

"What now?" Frank asked.

"Now I'm leaving and I'm taking Skye and Nico with me."

Frank laughed. "Nico belongs to me. The minute you leave I will call the police and have you arrested for kidnapping."

"What *legal* proof do you have that Nico is your son?"

Frank's smile faded and his gaze hardened. "He is my son."

"So prove it. And in the meantime it will take weeks to get a paternity test. By then, things will be a little more clear for everyone."

"You're a fool."

"Most likely," Christian agreed. "But I'm not leaving without them."

"I will ruin you," Frank Rocco said, almost casually but the fury in his eyes burned like banked coals. "I'll see to it that you never open so much as a grocery cart in this city if you walk out that door with what belongs to me."

Skye appeared, holding a sleepy Nico. She stared hard at Frank and moved to Christian's side. "Me and Nico are *people,* and we do not belong to anyone much less you, you disgusting pig."

"Brave words," Frank said, his mouth tipping in a tight smile. "We'll see how brave you are when I have you alone."

She suppressed a shudder but held her ground.

"I detest scenes," Frank said. "Get out of my house. But, Skye," he warned her with a glint in his eye that made Christian want to snuff it out, "this isn't settled. It has only begun."

Yeah. Somehow Christian didn't doubt that for a minute but the way he saw it—he didn't have a choice.

CHAPTER TWENTY-TWO

SKYE'S ENTIRE BODY SHOOK from nerves frazzled by adrenalin. Christian hadn't said a word aside from terse instructions to the cab driver as they left Belleni's. Nico was terrified, too. Everything in his world had changed in a short time frame.

"Are we going home?" he whispered.

"No, darling. We—" *Don't have a home any longer.* She risked a glance at Christian who ignored her but moved to ruffle Nico's hair softly.

"You're going to stay with me tonight until we figure out what's happening next. Is that okay with you?" he asked.

Nico nodded. "Can we go back to Thomas so he can teach me checkers?"

Christian didn't make promises but said, "We'll see."

"Christian—"

He shot her a warning look and she shrank away from the anger she saw there. She swallowed the lump in her throat and blinked away tears but she looked away so he wouldn't see her cry. Her pride burned but she had nowhere to go and for the time being, Christian was her sanctuary. Belleni would be looking for her tomorrow. She had to find a way out of the city before he found her.

They arrived at Christian's loft and took the short ride to his place. He opened the door for them and they walked in.

"I can take the couch with Nico," she said. "Do you have some blankets we could use?" She glanced down at her cream gown and grimaced. "And maybe something I could change into? I didn't exactly have a chance to grab any clothes before we left."

"Yeah," he said, but his expression hadn't softened. He went to his dresser and pulled out a pair of soft linen drawstring pants and a T-shirt for her.

"I'll figure something out tomorrow. I promise we won't be a burden for long," she said, accepting the clothes.

"What's a burden?" Nico asked, looking up at her with wide eyes.

She smoothed his brow and forced a smile. "Nothing for you to worry about, sweetheart. It's late and everything will look better in the morning."

She hoped.

Christian brought blankets and tossed them at her. She choked back the glare she wanted to give him and busied herself making a bed for Nico who was already yawning and struggling to stay awake.

Christian disappeared into the bathroom and she heard the water running. She sighed. She'd love a shower or a bath but that would have to wait. She had bigger problems than her need for a little quiet time.

She stroked Nico's soft hair until he fell fast asleep. His slow, even breathing soothed her jagged nerves but not her heart. The water shut off and she couldn't help but look toward the bathroom in the hopes of seeing Christian again, only this time with forgiveness in his eyes.

The door opened and Christian emerged, head damp, and dressed in sweats and a T-shirt. Again, he ignored her. The tiny hope she'd harbored died quickly and soundlessly. The smart thing would be to tuck herself into the blankets and allow sleep to wipe away her fear and turbulent thoughts but she couldn't let things sit the way they were without saying her piece. She eased away from Nico so as not to wake him and then padded silently to the four-poster bed where Christian was getting ready for bed. "Do you need something?" he asked curtly.

"Yes. I need to explain."

"Not necessary," he disagreed, dismissing her. She took a bold move and followed him, startling him as she climbed onto the bed with him, determined to have her say. "What are you doing?"

She ignored his question. "Everything the man you knew as Frank Rocco said was true," she started, her cheeks heating with shame. "Except there were parts he left out."

Christian settled against the pillows, his gaze hard. "Oh? And you feel like sharing, I see."

"You can be a jerk about this but I'm still going to tell you what happened so just shut up and give me the courtesy of at least listening. Afterward, you can do what you want."

"I'll do what I want regardless," he retorted.

She ignored the dig and drew a deep breath to continue. "Frank Rocco is also known as Belleni."

"You're a Belleni girl?" he asked and she nodded. Of course he'd heard about the Belleni girls.

"Yes. Not by choice," she added.

"Excuse me?"

"I have to start at the beginning otherwise it's hard to imagine how in this day and age someone could do this to another human being and get away with it. Belleni came to me shortly after my dance career ended. I was broken inside and maybe a little reckless. I was looking for a way to dull the pain and at first, he seemed the answer. He tricked me into thinking I could simply go on dates without any sex and make a good living. He was charming and protective and just the person I thought I needed. I thought I was in love with this kind, older gentleman. Then I got pregnant and everything changed. He became obsessed with me and started using Nico as leverage. He threatened to take Nico from me and when he found I'd been stockpiling money to get away from him, he had me beaten. He owned me. I was his slave as surely as if he had shackled me. I couldn't get out and couldn't get away without leaving Nico behind."

"What about your family in Iowa?" he asked.

She looked down at her fingers. "They don't know

what I've been doing for the past five years. They don't even know about Nico. I was too ashamed."

Christian's expression wavered, as if he were having a hard time believing her yet desperately wanted to. "Why didn't you tell me from the very beginning?"

"Tell you what? How was I supposed to tell a complete stranger that I was being held captive by a man who had more power than most politicians in this city? I'm sure that would've gone over well."

"Maybe not at first but—" He stopped, frustration lacing his tone then he gestured angrily. "How about when I was baring my soul to you by the creek? You had plenty of time at that point to level with me."

"I wanted to," she cried softly. "I truly did but I was afraid."

"Afraid?"

"Yes, afraid. Belleni is a dangerous man. I wasn't lying when I said the less you knew the safer you'd be. Belleni has secrets he would kill to keep safe. I couldn't put you and Mama Jo at risk like that."

"You didn't even give me the chance to decide for myself if it was a risk I was willing to take," he countered hotly.

"No, I didn't," she acknowledged. "But how was I supposed to know that things were going to turn out this way? My main concern was Nico. That's it." She blinked back tears. "I know you hate me right now. Because of me your biggest chance at opening a club is ruined. I'm not stupid. I lied to you, hell, you might even say I used you to get out of the city. But until you've walked a mile in my shoes don't judge me. You haven't a clue how much misery I've endured since making that one fatal mistake of trusting someone like Belleni."

Skye wiped away the moisture tracking down her cheeks and slid off the bed.

"So what now?" he asked, stopping her. "What happens to either of us?"

"I don't know," she murmured regretfully. "But there's one thing I know for sure…Belleni won't stop until he's made to stop. I can't stay here. Belleni owns my apartment and has confiscated all my money. The only thing I can do is try and go home. As for you, I'd say give it time, find a different venture capitalist but I'd be giving you false hope. He will set out to ruin you now. I'm sorry."

His expression fell and she could imagine the true weight of his decision was finally settling in and it was heavier than he imagined.

For that, and so much more, she was sorry.

BELLENI THREW THE DINNER KNIFE on the table with such force it stuck in the wall. How had the night disintegrated so quickly? Had he just allowed that miserable prick to walk away with his family? "Vivian!" He required action to fix this problem. No one stole from Belleni. Where is that woman? He bellowed her name again and she appeared framed in the doorway, looking as unruffled as ever, untouched by his personal crisis. "Did you know about them?" he demanded on a growl.

"Contrary to popular belief I am not infallible," Vivian said, moving to the marble-topped bar to fix a drink. "I guess you could say she pulled one over us. I didn't know until you knew." She lifted her shoulder in a shrug before sipping at her brandy. "How was dinner?" she asked, seemingly disinterested in the events that had just occurred.

Damn her, she was still sore at him. She wandered, drink in hand, to where the knife stuck rigidly and pulled it free. A faint look of disgust for the damage marked her face, but she refrained from commenting, which was just as well. Belleni wasn't in the mood to be chastised.

"Tomorrow, I want you to find out where he lives. Take two men and teach him how things work in this town. Then, call our contact in the city building inspections and ensure that no permit with his name on it ever gets cleared. I want to ruin him," Belleni said vehemently, closing his eyes against the rage that continued to simmer just beneath the surface. "I want him to return to me begging for a crumb from my table. And I want Skye brought home at all costs."

Vivian remained quiet as she returned to the bar. "You need to relax," she advised. "Your blood pressure is surely going through the roof. The doctor said you need to be mindful of your stress levels." He grunted something but he nodded. She was right, ranting and raving did nothing but foster sloppy thinking. He noticed with faint appreciation that Vivian was making him a drink. She smiled and put it into his hand. "Your favorite," she said simply.

He sighed and leaned back in the chair before shooting the rich, silky brown liquid down his throat, enjoying the smooth burn and the lingering aftertaste that coated his tongue. "Vivian, you are too good to me," he said at last, giving her an appreciative smile.

"I know," she acknowledged and he chuckled. "Another?"

He lifted his glass. "You know me well."

"That I do."

She refilled his glass and settled in the stiff-backed chair to his right. She was still a striking woman, he noted, fighting a sudden and pervasive fatigue. Cement weighted his eyelids and he struggled as his vision blurred. "Something…wrong…" he gasped, reaching out to Vivian for her help but she merely smiled. "Vivian…help me…"

"But I am, darling," she said with a patronizing tilt of her head. He stared in disbelief and she settled more comfortably in her chair as if to wait. And he knew.

"You've p-poisoned me?" She remained silent but her clear, chilly gaze answered loudly enough. "Why?" he demanded, his voice weakening as quickly as his body.

At that she leaned forward, her eyes flashing with all the banked fury she held inside and spat, "Because you had the audacity to think you could be rid of me so easily. As if the years between us simply evaporated because you got a sudden whim to play house. I have tolerated a lot but this—" she sank against the chair, her fingernail tapping the linen tablecloth "—was simply too much. How dare you throw me to the curb, *from my home,* like day-old garbage!" She took a moment to collect herself and then continued with a shrug. "I'll admit my first plan was to kill Skye and Nico but I realized they weren't the true problem…you were. Even if they weren't here, they would be in your heart and there would be nothing I could do to stop it. And I am nothing, if not efficient, wouldn't you say? I am rooting out the problem—you."

He struggled against the lethargy that was stealing his strength and sapping his mental clarity. "I take it back, you can live here as long as you like," he promised with a slight slur. Black dots danced at the edges of his vision. "I love you, darling, I always have. There is no one who can ever replace you!" he exclaimed in desperation.

"I know." She placed her hand on her chest in a gentle motion. "And there is no one who will ever replace you in my heart. I will remember our time fondly." She rose and pressed a sweet kiss to his slack lips before walking away.

The last image Belleni ever saw was Vivian's slim backside as she left him behind to die—alone.

CHAPTER TWENTY-THREE

CHRISTIAN AWOKE THE NEXT morning to find Skye and Nico gone. He couldn't say he was surprised but he cursed out loud just the same.

He supposed she'd called her family and they'd wired her some money to get back to Iowa. He didn't envy her homecoming after all these years. In fact, he couldn't stop the twinge of concern for her in spite of everything.

Hell, who was he kidding? It was more than a twinge. It hurt like hell. His chest felt caved in, as though someone's foot was lodged where his heart beat.

He scrubbed the sleep from his eyes and climbed from the bed. Skye had left their blankets folded neatly, an attempt, he supposed, to minimize the trouble she left behind in some small way.

He grabbed the top blanket and brought it to his nose to inhale deeply. It smelled faintly of Skye's shampoo. The pain in his chest increased and he dropped the blanket back to the sofa.

He ought to call Gage, clean up some of this mess but frankly, he didn't know what to say. Gage probably didn't want to see him right about now anyway.

How had everything turned to shit so quickly? Talk about blindsided.

He needed to focus, fix one problem at a time. He grabbed his cell phone and dialed Thomas. His brother answered after the first ring. He didn't waste time on frivolities. "I got a problem," he stated, going right to the point.

"Yeah? What's wrong?"

Christian took a deep breath and then spilled it all.

"What about Skye?" Thomas asked gravely.

"What about her? She's gone. For all I know she could be halfway to the cornfields of Iowa by now." Was that bitterness in his voice? Yeah, he was fairly certain it was. "Listen, I just want to make sure she's safe."

"It's not really your problem at this point," Thomas said.

"It feels like it is. I can't walk away until I know she's okay. Then, she's on her own."

"You sure?"

"Yeah," he said dully. "I'm sure."

"You got it. I'll call as soon as I know something," Thomas said on a sigh. "Maybe you ought to come home for a few weeks, let things settle before you head back to the city," he suggested.

"I can't, I have work. But I'll be fine."

"Okay. I'll be in touch. I'm here if you need anything."

Thomas hung up and Christian went to grab some breakfast but a knock at the door caught his attention. His heart rate leaped at the hope that it might be Skye and Nico but when he opened the door and saw the woman Skye called Vivian, he stiffened and was tempted to slam the door in her face.

"May I come in?" she asked, removing her sunglasses and stepping inside without waiting for an invitation. Her gaze roved the loft and faint appreciation lit her eyes. "Not bad," she noted with an air of disdain.

"What do you want? If this is about last night, you can tell your employer my brother works for the FBI and he's already looking into his business so he better back off. And leave Skye alone."

Vivian smiled but it seemed more perfunctory than genuine and he didn't know what to think of it until she rooted in her purse and pulled a thick envelope. "Give this to Skye, please," she instructed. "Inside is the money Belleni took from her, all ten thousand dollars plus a small additional amount for her trouble. It's all she'll ever see from Belleni so she can forget about asking for more."

"I doubt Skye wants anything from him," he retorted, accepting the envelope reluctantly. He didn't even know where Skye was, and it didn't feel quite right to take the money. "Why don't you give this to her yourself?"

"I have better things to do than chase after Skye. I've gladly washed my hands of her now that Belleni has died."

"Died?"

"Yes. He died of a heart attack late last night, no doubt from the strain of the evening. Neither Nico nor Skye are in the will. Everything goes to me."

"Nico is Belleni's son, though," Christian said.

Vivian's gaze hardened. "There is no evidence stating as such. He is not listed on the birth certificate nor was there any formal recognition."

"There's always DNA."

She seemed annoyed, exasperated by the topic of conversation when she clearly wanted to move on. "Am I to understand that you are not interested in being with Skye and her brat?"

"Watch your mouth, lady," he warned. "And that's none of your business."

"True," she conceded, returning to the discussion at hand. "Give this message to Skye—this is all she'll ever get from the estate. Don't come looking for more," she repeated in warning. Christian had never seen a more cold, calculating person than the one standing before him. And just like that, her mood changed to one more pleasant as she said, "There is one more thing...if you're still interested in opening the nightclub, I might be interested in stepping in as the new silent partner. I've always wanted to own my own club." She handed him her card. "Call me if you're interested."

"Listen, I don't know where to find Skye. It wouldn't be right—"

"Keep the money, burn it, give it to her, I don't really care. The burden of Skye D'Lane is no longer my concern. I never want to see her or her brat ever again. Are we clear, Mr. Holt?"

Vivian didn't wait for an answer. She opened the door and let herself out. He stared at the thick envelope and fought an internal battle. He knew he had to talk to her, tell her about the money as well as share the news about Belleni but he wasn't quite ready to do either of those things. He needed time to clear his head. Focus.

What had started out as a genuine desire to help someone get out of a bad situation had morphed into something he didn't even recognize any longer. When he first looked at Skye all he saw was the prostitution and the sordid reality of her profession. It smacked too closely to the pain of living with the memories of his mother. But slowly, he'd started to see *her.* And that's when things started to slip out of his control.

He could've kept his mouth shut and walked away with the keys to his dreams.

But that would've condemned Skye to a nightmare.

Now he didn't have the girl or the club.

He wanted to put his fist through the wall. What

he wouldn't do for a cord of wood to start hacking on.

The fact of the matter was he couldn't quite see himself walking away, but then how did he reconcile the fact of her previous lifestyle and her deception? Truthfully, he could probably forgive the prostitution—with time—hell, everyone had stuff in their closets they wanted to forget. But the lies—why couldn't she have leveled with him about her situation? He would've rather found out about Frank Rocco/Belleni before sitting at the man's table—ate him, and each time he tried to move past it, it stuck in his craw.

He wanted to believe that he could've handled the truth. Skye hadn't even given him the opportunity to rise to the occasion. She'd made an assumption of his reaction and that rubbed him wrong. He suppressed a groan of frustration. Everything about this situation rubbed him raw and bloody.

He grabbed his cell but didn't dial. He held on to that phone as if it were his lifeline. He didn't have the answers. Not yet. But he had something he had to do. He dialed her number and it went to voice mail, not that he expected anything different.

"I know you don't want to talk to me but it's important. I'm hoping you haven't hitched a plane back to Iowa just yet because it's going to take some hunting around to find you among the great corn state but I need to talk to you. I have something for you that you're going to want. Meet me at the park today at two o'clock. I hope you're there."

Now, he could only follow through and hope she was there, too.

SKYE LISTENED TO THE MESSAGE twice. She chewed her bottom lip, not quite sure what to do. What could he possibly have for her that would be so important he'd chase her down? That question alone was enough to compel her to meet him at the park but there was a small voice in the back of her head that warned her to stay away. Seeing him again would only pour salt in the wound.

Against her better judgment she and Nico caught a cab to the park. She allowed Nico to run to the swings while she took a seat on a park bench. She'd managed to slip back into her old apartment and find some clothes that hadn't been packed by the movers yet and even grabbed a few things of Nico's but they had to travel light so she left behind a lot.

As crappy as her existence had been and the apartment was hardly the epitome of living large, it'd been her sanctuary.

Lost in her thoughts, she didn't realize Christian was beside her until he reached out and touched her shoulder. She jumped and when she saw it was him, she tried not to show how much she wished things were different between them.

"I'm glad you came," he said.

"Well, you said it was important," she replied

stiffly. God, why did it hurt so much just to be near him? This love crap was for the birds, she thought to herself. Love? Yes, she thought with a sinking heart. She'd gone and fallen in love with the man and he likely couldn't stand her. "What is so important that you couldn't just tell me over the phone?"

He reached behind him and pulled out a fat envelope. "Well, for one, it's hard to pass a wad of money through the phone and two, I needed to see you before you disappeared."

She stared at the envelope, not quite understanding, but when he insisted that she take it, she did with great reluctance. In her experience big sums of cash didn't just fall into your lap without strings attached. "What are you talking about?"

He gestured to the spot beside her. "May I?"

"I suppose," she allowed, scooting just a little to give them more space. She opened the envelope to peek inside. Holy hell. She gaped at Christian. "There's got to be thousands of dollars in here. What's going on?"

"That skinny, creepy woman that hustled you and Nico out of Mama Jo's showed up at my loft this morning. I don't even want to know how she knew where I lived but, anyway, she shows up with this envelope saying it belonged to you. She said it's ten thousand plus a little extra for your trouble."

"That's how much Belleni took from me," she murmured, unable to believe it was now clutched in her hands. "How? Why?" She had too many questions. "What else did she say?"

"For one, she said that Frank Rocco/Belleni, whatever name he goes by, is dead."

"What?"

"Yeah. I don't know all the details, don't really care to know the details, but suffice to say he's not going to be chasing you down for custody anytime soon."

She nearly sagged with relief and if she was judged for being thankful of Belleni's death so be it. "And Vivian brought you the money, just like that?"

"Not exactly. She said you are no longer her burden. She doesn't like you very much," he added.

"No, she doesn't," Skye agreed, still reeling from the news. "Was that all?"

"In essence, but I have some bad news. Nico isn't going to inherit any of Belleni's money or assets. According to Slim, everything goes to her because there's no proof that Belleni had any heirs. You could get a DNA sample and take her to court—"

"No, thank you," she breathed, becoming giddy with relief. It was over. "God, I've dreamed of this day but I never truly thought I'd live to see it." She closed her eyes briefly and whispered, "Thank you, Vivian." Even though she was under no false illusions as to Vivian's motivation, it freed her just the same and she'd take it any way she could get it.

She knew her eyes were sparkling when Christian's gaze locked on to hers and seemed to get lost in her unadulterated joy for a moment. "I don't think I'll ever get tired of seeing your beautiful face," he murmured, his stare turning serious.

She startled at his statement, afraid she'd heard him wrong. "What do you mean?"

He took a risk and reached out to caress her face. "You know what sucks about knee-jerk reactions?" he asked and she shook her head. "You usually end up nailing yourself in the face and feeling pretty stupid about it afterward," he answered with a soft grin.

"Are you saying, you didn't mean what you said earlier?"

"No. Yes. Well, sort of." Christian sighed, pulling away. "Skye, I can forgive you for the things you had to do for survival. I know all about that having watched my mom. What killed me was the lies. If you had leveled with me from the beginning—"

"You would've walked," Skye cut in flatly. Then she looked away, adding with a shrug, "But I should've told you anyway. You're right. It'd been so long since I'd done anything resembling normal I craved just a taste with you. I wanted to pretend that I was like anyone else, free to date, to experience a relationship because I wanted to, not because someone was paying me. But it wasn't right and I'm sorry I dragged you into a mess."

"I get it, I do. I just wish you could've trusted me a little more," he said.

She nodded. "Me, too."

They held each other's gaze as the open air

cleansed the wound festering between them and then Christian reached out and gently pulled her to him. She didn't resist and tears pricked her eyes as he pressed his lips to hers in a tender kiss that spoke volumes to her heart.

"I feel there's something special between us, Skye," he said as the kiss ended. "And I don't want to see this end until we know we've taken it as far as it can go."

"No matter where it takes us?" she asked, a bit fearfully. "What if it ends up in a small house with a fenced yard in West Virginia or Iowa for that matter? I don't think I can live in the city much longer, Christian," she admitted. "There are too many memories, and most of them I'm ashamed of."

"I'm not afraid," he said, and he meant it. He realized in that moment that he'd follow Skye anywhere she wanted to go.

"What about your nightclub deal?" she asked, not quite ready to trust in the good fortune. "And your plans for the warehouse? You've already invested so much of your time and money on that particular spot."

"I haven't given up," Christian said. "Hey, I've got Vivian wanting to be a silent partner." Skye's eyes widened and she gave a minute shake of her head causing him to laugh. "Don't worry, I'm not taking her up on the offer but it made me think. Hey, if I can get two people interested, I can get another two people and if those don't pan out, I'll just keep going until I do. There's another perfect spot out there somewhere. I just have to find it. I'll open the club somehow and maybe it's not here in the city but somewhere else." He gazed at her meaningfully. "Like somewhere within driving distance of a small house with a fenced yard."

"Do you mean it? Don't play with me if you're not serious," she warned, sucking back a watery cry.

Christian sobered and she knew he was speaking from the heart when he said, "I've never been so sure about anything else in my life. Skye D'Lane, I want to build a life with you and I'll take you any way I can get you. I want to make babies and raise Nico with you. And I know this is the real deal because I've never felt like this about anyone in my entire life. If you'd said two years ago I was going to fall in love and want to settle down I'd have told you you were crazy but here I am, ready and eager, as long as it's you I'm doing it with. All I ask is that we stay long enough for me to get Mathias through baseball season and then we'll figure things out."

"I think that's doable," she said, smiling. "And in the meantime I'll teach dance at the group home if they'll take me back."

"Sounds like a plan," he said, the corners of his luscious mouth curving in a warm smile. "I'm sorry," he added, causing her to frown.

"Sorry?"

He ducked his gaze but then said, "I'm sorry I wasn't able to see who you are. I was too caught up in who you *were* to take that chance. And I'm sorry I didn't do anything to keep you from getting into that limo. For the rest of my life I'll regret it."

Tears streamed down her face and she didn't try to stop them. She cupped his face. "Don't waste another moment on regret. Mama Jo said everything happens for a reason. Maybe she's right. I'm here now and Belleni is out of our lives for good. I've put my life on hold for the past five years. I'm ready to start living again."

"Sounds like the best damn news I've ever heard," Christian murmured, leaning over to press a soft, sweet kiss on her lips that made her toes curl in the nicest way.

She never dared to hope that someday she'd find a man as kind, strong and amazing as Christian but here he was and she wasn't going to turn him away. She was going to love him for the rest of her life and give him lots of babies to hold and adore and she was going to watch with pride as Nico learned how to be a man under Christian's guiding hand.

But first, she had one more thing to tell him…

She smiled up at him and caressed his beloved face, taking in every minute detail so that when she closed her eyes she could always find him in her mind and then whispered her final secret into his ear.

"My name's not really Skye D'Lane. It's Mary Jane Hosker." She giggled when he stared in astonishment and then she shrugged. "What can I say…I'm a farmer's daughter from Iowa, remember?"

"Come here, whoever the hell you are," he growled, grabbing her to pull her squealing into his arms and she knew it didn't matter what he called her as long as he said it with love for the rest of their lives.

* * * * *

One more of Mama Jo's boys is ready
to meet his match!
Be sure to look for Owen's story,
SECRETS IN A SMALL TOWN!

Harlequin® SuperRomance®

COMING NEXT MONTH

Available May 10, 2011

#1704 A FATHER'S QUEST
Spotlight on Sentinel Pass
Debra Salonen

#1705 A TASTE OF TEXAS
Hometown U.S.A.
Liz Talley

#1706 SECRETS IN A SMALL TOWN
Mama Jo's Boys
Kimberly Van Meter

#1707 THE PRODIGAL SON
Going Back
Beth Andrews

#1708 AS GOOD AS HIS WORD
More Than Friends
Susan Gable

#1709 MITZI'S MARINE
In Uniform
Rogenna Brewer

HSRCNM0411

With an evil force hell-bent on destruction, two enemies must unite to find a truth that turns all-too-personal when passions collide.

Enjoy a sneak peek in Jenna Kernan's next installment in her original TRACKER *series, GHOST STALKER, available in May, only from Harlequin Nocturne.*

"Who are you?" he snarled.

Jessie lifted her chin. "Your better."

His smile was cold. "Such arrogance could only come from a Niyanoka."

She nodded. "Why are you here?"

"I don't know." He glanced about her room. "I asked the birds to take me to a healer."

"And they have done so. Is that *all* you asked?"

"No. To lead them away from my friends." His eyes fluttered and she saw them roll over white.

Jessie straightened, preparing to flee, but he roused himself and mastered the momentary weakness. His eyes snapped open, locking on her.

Her heart hammered as she inched back.

"Lead who away?" she whispered, suddenly afraid of the answer.

"The ghosts. Nagi sent them to attack me so I would bring them to her."

The wolf must be deranged because Nagi did not send ghosts to attack living creatures. He captured the evil ones after their death if they refused to walk the Way of Souls, forcing them to face judgment.

"Her? The healer you seek is also female?"

"Michaela. She's Niyanoka, like you. The last Seer of Souls and Nagi wants her dead."

HNEXP0511

Jessie fell back to her seat on the carpet as the possibility of this ricocheted in her brain. Could it be true?

"Why should I believe you?" But she knew why. His black aura, the part that said he had been touched by death. Only a ghost could do that. But it made no sense.

Why would Nagi hunt one of her people and why would a Skinwalker want to protect her? She had been trained from birth to hate the Skinwalkers, to consider them a threat.

His intent blue eyes pinned her. Jessie felt her mouth go dry as she considered the impossible. Could the trickster be speaking the truth? Great Mystery, what evil was this?

She stared in astonishment. There was only one way to find her answers. But she had never even met a Skinwalker before and so did not even know if they dreamed.

But if he dreamed, she would have her chance to learn the truth.

HNEXP0511